Dark sun

EDGARS AUZIŅŠ

Published by EDGARS AUZIŅŠ, 2024.

This is a work of fiction. Similarities to real people, places, or events are entirely coincidental.

DARK SUN

First edition. June 2, 2024.

ISBN: 979-8227129611

Written by EDGARS AUZIŅŠ.

Part 1

Now.

- Don't get attached. Throw love into the fire, otherwise it will only bring you sadness, her mother told her.

-You will have many lives. People like us are destined to spend eternity on earth. Someday you will forget your first name, although its ghost will always remain with you. And your native land will become a foreign and distant land to you, not awakening memories in your soul, no matter how much you try to preserve them. You will lie with men, some of them will be able to awaken feelings in you, but the next cycle will sweep them into the Abyss without a trace. You will learn that in life, bright feelings pass away most quickly, gratitude is forgotten, and sincere deeds and victories are consigned to oblivion. But one thing, alas, always remains with us - our deaths. You will remember them, every single one. Just like those who kill you...

Gilota, Gilda's only daughter, died for the first time when she was sixteen years old. This happened due to a long, serious illness in which the entire village perished, and Gilota forever retained the memory of clothes soaked from feverish sweat, a hard straw mattress, the stench of bodies decomposing in the sun, which there was no one to clean up. When she woke up again, lying in her underwear on the dewy grass and looking at the sky filling with pink light, her mother was no longer nearby. Then she cried a little, realizing that she would never see her again. Then she wiped away her tears, got up and walked wherever she could. Tiny sparks flickered on her fingertips all morning, but then she pulled herself together and took control of the power.

"People like us," my mother said, "are destined for eternal loneliness. It is too dangerous for us to be close to our own kind, and mortals flash before our eyes and disappear into the Abyss. You'll get used to it one day. "Alas, we, like mortals, are capable of yearning and cannot avoid disappointment."

Seven hours after the start of her first cycle, Gilota killed a man. It was an ordinary traveler who had his eye on a lonely girl wandering along the side of the road. Gilota burned out his eyes and took the wallet to acquire personal belongings in the nearest city. With the onset of darkness, the wolves came to the blinded cripple and finished off what she did not want to get her hands dirty on. But she considered him as the first.

She had times when she had to kill a lot, and there were months, years, decades of quiet life when she used the Force only for good. But it all ended the same way - one day she herself was killed, and the cycle began again. Short lives were quickly erased from memory; she learned to preserve long and fruitful ones longer.

Gilota managed to first love her past life with all her heart, then hate and curse it. And last night she had a dream, one of those dreams that never come in vain. In Gilote's dream, her past death appeared.

In her sleep, Eternal Empress Orecia knelt down, pressing her hands to her bloody stomach. The corset of a luxurious dress embroidered with black pearls was mercilessly ripped open by a blade, thick braids scattered over the shoulders like a dark cloak. Oresia watched the last sparks under her palms die out and thought about how blind and arrogant she had been just a few moments ago. The fatal blow, so likely, still struck her suddenly. Now time has stopped. And things went differently. Heavy drops fell, measuring the approach of the Abyss, like the last grains of sand in a clock.

"Strong, very strong," said the man standing above her, and she expected to find mockery in his voice, but there was only fatigue. "I was proud that men weren't given this." But what, creature from the darkness, have I now managed to surprise you?

Oresia could no longer answer. She felt the enemy lower his sword, and it fell with a ringing sound onto the stone slabs of the floor. A crumpled helmet followed. Oresia raised her eyes, and for the last time glanced over the blood-soaked and darkened cloak, over the spattered hem of her shirt, over the singed and torn chain mail, and higher, to the smoky face, on which the eyes burned with two icy sparks, in which the flash of power was now gradually fading away. The enemy was also wounded. She managed to understand this, seeing how a new scarlet stain was spreading on her shirt. She was able to get it too.

And then the man lifted Orecia, wrapping her hair around his fist, and cut her throat. Quickly, without any pleasure, he fulfilled his sacred duty. Drenched in blood, he grabbed her and lowered her to the floor. With dirty fingers he lowered his eyelids... and froze a few moments longer than he should have. For some reason I looked into his face. Only then did the man cover his body with a cloak and wander away, towards the exit of the hall. He constantly had to step over bodies. There was a loud squelching sound under the soles of his boots, as if he were walking through a swamp.

Gilota woke up without a cry, and didn't even flinch. She simply opened her eyes and looked at the ceiling, hung with a canopy made from old colorful scarves, as she once looked at the dawn sky.

She lowered her feet to the floor and stretched sweetly. In the room that served as her bedroom and the only personal refuge on the floor, darkness reigned, and behind the thick velvet curtains the sun was already rising, she always felt this unmistakably.

Today her name is Almasina, but some prefer it simply - Sage. She is not offended, she is even proud somewhere deep down. Now her possessions are small - a rented laboratory on the second floor of an old house, with windows overlooking the square. Once upon a time, the Eternal Empress Oresia stood sculptured in stone on a stone pedestal, but ten years ago, a maddened crowd smashed the sculpture into small fragments. Now, beggars gather in the shade of the high pedestal on hot summer days. They sit on the filthy sidewalk, lie there, eat there, copulate and relieve themselves there, not forgetting to annoyingly beg for alms from random passers-by who are in a hurry to cross the crappy square at a fast pace. Just recently this would have been unimaginable;

now it's enough just to go to the window and pull back the heavy curtains. The Witch does not like daylight, although it has no power to harm her, so the curtains are always drawn tightly. She also prefers not to think about the bad.

During the day, townspeople and villagers who have come from far away come to her to take blessings and conspiracies, predictions and warnings, dried herbs and roots, decoctions and ointments. And also leave spirit-induced illness, sadness or misfortune, or unwanted offspring in the stomach. This is her part of the world, so far the only one worthy of attention. Sorceress Almasina gives and receives, for the first time in many years the power does not burn out the immortal Gilota from the inside. She still remembers what it's like to be empty. But now she's happy. Her feelings told her that a good day was coming. Something very important will happen, you just need to read the invisible signs of power in time.

* * *

Seven years ago.

"I have always been amazed by the fragility of the human body. And the unbending firmness of what finds a temporary home in him," said the black brother. "If only I could find a blacksmith who could melt such a soul in a forge and turn it into a blade..."

However, the black brother did not finish his thought, and again looked searchingly at the man sitting in the chair. He bowed his head, his lips moving silently. Either he was praying, or he was sending death curses. However, the black brother was not afraid of the latter. He and the venerable commission at the table were reliably protected. The man was kept, as befits a filthy sorcerer - in a collar and shackles, whose sacred pattern locked the cursed power. In addition, he was once physically strong, and therefore even now thick belts and iron fastenings kept him motionless drawn to the torture chair. You can't even turn your head in the clamps.

Four hours today, eight yesterday, like all last week. And only powerless curses, vile blasphemy and dirty curses. The black brother suggested that the head of the commission burn out the bastard's tongue with his own hands, but for some reason he undertook to follow the formalities to the end. It became easier when the damned sorcerer lost his voice.

The head of the commission repeated the question. The black brother is already bored with counting how many times this has happened, so he habitually bent down and slightly turned two levers in the mechanism. Experience told me that there were only a few moments left until the incomparable crunch.

"You won't have a left hand," he told the man. "When the pressure becomes extreme, both bones will burst, and the fragments will pierce the muscles. The important thing here is how quickly the doctor gets down to business. But they won't call him for you, because you are not contributing to the investigation. Until there is a sign from you, no one will meet you halfway. If you are stupid, they will cut off your hand later.

He leaned over to make sure he was heard. But the man made no attempt to say anything or move.

The head of the commission made a sign to one of the guards, and he left. The black brother watched carefully and saw that the man was alarmed and wary. The first sign of interest in the world around me in a long time. And when the guard returned with another one, and the man saw what they were dragging behind them...

Falco was fourteen years old, and he was proud that Sir Thomas Wyatt had accepted him as his squire. Now, when the naked, bound boy was dragged into the interrogation room, only horror was visible in his face. While the head of the commission read out the resolution, which sounded like a complete verdict, the boy stared at the owner, unable to take his eyes off the disfigured body. Probably, if it weren't for the gag, squire Falko screamed immediately. As it was, he just clenched his teeth when he was strapped into a chair opposite his owner. The man's gaze did not change, and the black brother worriedly thought that he had missed something important. And then the man opened his mouth and let out a series of inaudible wheezes.

- He has nothing to do with it, he is not to blame. What are you doing? — the black brother translated for himself.

"We are establishing the truth," said the head of the commission. "If not the criminal himself, then his servant and accomplice can help us discover the truth."

The chairs were installed in such a way as to exclude the commission from the field of view of the defendants, but the man still tried to move his head and shifted his gaze as far as he could. He wheezed again.

"He doesn't know anything," the black brother recognized.

- But you know.

The man closed his eyes. At a sign from the head of the commission, the black brother pulled on his gloves and took pliers from the grill.

"A metal burn has several stages," the black brother spoke. - The first one is safe.

And without any tricks he applied the red-hot pliers to the boy's wrist, just above the fastening belt. There was a scream. The black brother put the tongs back on the brazier. He turned and saw that the man was looking at the boy writhing in pain. Not a muscle moved on his face, but a hoarse, incomprehensible voice said:

- I'll sign. No need. Put it down.

The head of the commission nodded. The secretary immediately brought him a pile of paper covered in cramped handwriting and a pen and inkwell. The black brother slightly loosened the belt on his right wrist. The man slowly moved his hand with twisted, nailless fingers.

"Let him go," he repeated. - Now. And I will sign everything.

- You have no right to order the state commission. Your signature is just the first step towards cooperation.

The black brother read from the man's face that he understood everything. With a rather tenacious glance, he snatched out the dry lines of the protocol and examined the ingenious investigative mechanism awaiting ahead. But he had no way out.

Either sign or watch.

However, the first option did not cancel the second at all, he realized this and looked at the boy again. Young Falco mumbled something through his gag, probably trying to tell his master that knightly honor is a very expensive thing, more expensive than any squire. In the memory of the black brother, they all first said something like this. But the master-sorcerer was reasonable, he understood that then there would be no loyalty to the master, but only pain.

The man clutched his pen. It was not firm enough, and the tip trembled violently, as did his hands, leaving no doubt that he would not be able to write a single letter. But all that was important here was that it was the hand of Sir Thomas Wyatt who touched the paper with ink in the presence of the commission and witnesses. He signed the first confession.

The secretary sprinkled sand on the ink. The head of the commission reviewed the signed protocol and made a new instruction with a gesture.

"Get it over with," the black brother translated to himself.

He put his gloves back on.

- Before we move on to the next questions...

The man jerked so hard that the fastenings groaned. And he even tried to scream, but a distorted animal howl escaped from his throat. A familiar crunching sound was heard - the defendant had tensed up too much. But he clearly wasn't screaming from pain, not only from it. And the black brother realized with amazement that he had underestimated the snake witch's nature. The man in the chair deliberately misled them by pretending to be half dead. And now he lost his cool and immediately gave himself away. He was hooked tightly, now he won't break free, he won't hide.

The black brother thought that no powerful blacksmith was needed. He himself is a great craftsman, now he will pull this damned hard soul out of a man, crush it into powder, and scatter it to the wind.

"Well, you degenerate of darkness, have we managed to surprise you now?"

The look of the faded, once blue eyes changed only for a moment, as if the man looked inside himself, but then returned to reality. The black brother could not read this feeling. He had more important things to do. The next time he applied the red-hot pliers to the boy's shoulder, feeling complete satisfaction from his own work.

* * *

Now

This slave did not have a name. The definition of "this" was enough for the owner and his servants to understand what they were talking about.

Before dawn, this one opened his eyes and turned his head to look at the sky through the bars of the cage. He was sure that a few moments ago he was dreaming. Centuries-old crowns of trees intertwined overhead, grass flooded with water underfoot. He walked along it slowly and carefully. He didn't want to go, but for some reason he had no choice. This one walked, and the water rose. Now it was overflowing his knees, and he hesitated, trying to shake off the sticky obsession and turn away. Something in the water wrapped around his ankle and tugged. This one clenched his teeth and, without even uttering a frightened cry, fell into the water. Slippery vines moved there, they first wrapped around his legs, then grabbed his arms, desperately rushing in search of support. They entangled his body, hips, shoulders, neck, not allowing him to move, and then this one clearly realized that he was about to die.

"Don't be afraid," whispered a gentle voice.

"Fear not, brave knight. After all, you were once not afraid of anything, or it just seemed so to me. But still, don't be afraid now. What do you have to fear while I'm in front of you and holding my fingers in sight?"

An invisible force tied him hand and foot, and held him under water, not allowing him to escape. But he saw that the light overhead was slowly receding, primeval darkness was closing in around him, and something was still pulling his helpless body to the depths, not releasing its suffocating grip.

This one knew that the Abyss does not send such dreams in vain. Something must happen. Today, or maybe only tomorrow. But it will be something bad, maybe even terrible. I haven't seen any other option here. He could only sit in the cage and wait for it to overtake him. Feel it coming.

When they brought him a bowl of thin stew - already a familiar breakfast - he learned that the owner had decided to sell him.

Part 2

On the first day of the fair, when there were too many people on the street, the merchant Goslin was spending his leisure time looking at the dressed-up passers-by hurrying past his tiny dusty window, when a girl suddenly knocked on the door of the shop. Goslin looked at her through the glass and grinned. He thought she wouldn't come again. Well, since she showed up... Goslin got out from behind the counter and pulled back the bolt.

-What are you doing, mister? - the girl was surprised.

- Yes, they go...

Visitors irritated him, they disturbed the comfortable silence of his small dusty abode, asked stupid questions, pretended to be sages and experts. And this girl seems to be nothing at all. She is as tall as Goslin's shoulder, and maybe even shorter; who can tell these women with their ringing heels. Dressed in a simple black dress covered with a cloak. On her shoulder lay a heavy dark braid with a thin emerald ribbon. The face is pale, the gaze is too intent. With this look she greeted the pride of the shop - the skull of a devilish boar, according to legend for visitors, personally obtained in the southern forests. The skull bared fangs, each a finger long and two fingers thick.

-Did you get it?

- Goslin will get everything that no one else can get!

- Philosopher's stone, unicorn horn? — the girl immediately clarified.

"But I charge three times the price for very smart people," Goslin grinned.

From under the counter he took out a small bundle of black fabric and red threads; the girl seemed to extend her hand, but he held the goods with his palm.

"I asked knowledgeable people," he stated emphatically. "It turned out that their knowledge is not complete in everything." Only one answered me. He is over a hundred years old, and only once, in his youth, did he seem to have heard from his teacher that this could happen. He suggested where to find it. Why would you need something that you cannot handle?

The girl seemed nervous. She folded her hands and began to twirl the heavy ring with a red stone on her finger.

- What makes you think that I can't handle it? To stir water in a pot, you don't need either age-old wisdom or great strength. I also had good teachers. But if the question is not idle, knowledge costs money. So how much does it cost me?

Goslin didn't know what to think about this. Knowledge, that's how. If the girl really got hold of a couple of recipes that had long since sunk into time, this could now make a fortune. There are all sorts of amateurs, practitioners, salon "sorcerers", and they are all ready to pay a lot of money even for useless rubbish and empty words. But there are others, serious people, and they will reward you adequately for a real treasure. Just not to miss the thread that will lead him to the right path.

"Twenty dinars," he said.

The girl just raised her eyebrows in surprise and began to unlace her fanny pack.

"A small discount for future cooperation," said Goslin, and immediately realized that it was in vain. She herself understood everything, because she took out not only the wallet, but also a tiny token, and put it in his palm along with the silver coins.

Gilota slipped out of the shop, holding the edge of her cloak so as not to get caught in the door, and immediately heard the bolt clanging behind her again. Extra people never crossed the old, chipped threshold of the shop. But her owner could hardly tolerate even the necessary ones. If it wasn't about big money. Here the gloomy bottom fish swallowed the bait right away, without even thinking whether it was really hungry.

She had no doubt that Goslin would come to the meeting. And a moment later she threw it out of her head and disappeared into the loitering crowd.

* * *

The city of Recknitz once stood on a high hill, surrounded by two impregnable walls. It was a fortress, the home of the feudal lord Akerlea and his entourage. The inner circle is in the center, under reliable protection, and in the ring between the fortress walls is the housing of commoners, artisans, and laborers. The same family owned the fortress and the surrounding lands until the venerable Emperor left this joyless world, leaving on the throne his wife, the once rootless witch Oresia, who appeared as if from nowhere.

The Emperor's wife, who had accepted the crown of marriage as a young maiden, had not changed in ten years of marriage, and Akerlea watched with a carefully hidden grin as a pale girl in mourning clothing appeared in the meeting room to fulfill the duty of her deceased husband and head the military council. She was so short in stature, she was lost behind the shoulders of the personal guard soldiers accompanying her. And when the Emperor's widow sat at the head of the table, Akerlea allowed himself to stand up and publicly declare that he was an experienced warrior and would lose his honor if he allowed himself to take instructions from a woman. Empress Oresia did not answer him, she just looked somehow too intently. And those who were sitting closer managed to notice that time had nevertheless changed her face, it was not now the face of a young maiden, not at all. Later, the courtiers argued about what first flared up and took up the bright scarlet flame - the clothes of the feudal lord Akerlea or his body itself.

Later, Gilota recalled with a grin that the spectacular gesture cost her too much. For the next three months, she was more powerless than an ordinary person. But this event was the beginning. Everything that happened next is the era that the citizens of the empire now call "the time of the Dark Sun." The era of tyranny of the Eternal Empress Oresia.

Over the course of a hundred years, the town of Recknitz has changed. During the years of peace, people began to settle behind the fortress walls, on the plain, no longer fearing raids from neighboring lands. This is how the first settlements appeared, gradually becoming overgrown with new settlers' houses, shops, taverns, and dens. The fortress of the old city could be seen on the hill, a black stone mass towering above the branching streets and houses of the new city running off into the horizon. And somewhere in its midst, in front of one of the many squares, where there was now nothing remarkable, stood the house of the Sorceress Almasina.

There was unprecedented excitement in the streets and squares. A roar of voices, screams, and the clatter of hooves could be heard. The sidewalks were filled with assorted people at dawn. On foot, on horseback, in richly decorated carriages, on shabby carts, legless in carts... Clever beggars scurried through the crowd every now and then - look more carefully, and hold on to things so as not to be torn out of your hands. Rich clothes, rags, costumes of artisans and workers, clean faces, dirty faces and unimaginable ugliness flashed by.

Crowds streamed across the city to a dozen squares, where fairground tents were now erected and hastily put together booths erected. The Mid-Autumn Festival, loud and long-awaited, was on its first day and was only gaining momentum.

It seemed that you didn't even have to look for landmarks in the interweaving of streets - the crowd carried Gilota itself, like a deep river splashing in a deep gorge between dusty facades. The houses stretched upward, topped with plank superstructures, and she looked up, where curious faces leaned out of the windows, laundry was drying, the smells of cooking food could be heard, and at any moment slop or the contents of someone's chamber pot could splash out on the heads of passers-by.

The music of orchestras and mechanical organs rushed over the fair, merging into a single cacophony, thousands of voices boomed incessantly, barkers shouted loudly. The goods are laid out randomly and after goat's milk and cheese they sell bright clay toys, wicker baskets, pumpkins, worn-out shoes and copper basins. It took a lot of effort to find the right tents and stalls every time.

Gilota dived under the dark canopy, into the thick aroma of forbs, and came back out, already hiding a bundle tied with twine in her belt bag. A peasant passed by, dragging a well-groomed red cow on a rope, its hooves lazily smacking through the trampled mud. In the willow-wicker cage, the thin-faced dogs began to cry deafeningly. When Gilota passed by, the animals fell silent for a few moments and followed her with their gazes, but no one really noticed.

She even liked wandering in the crowd. Glimpse into faces, look at counters hung with patchwork carpets or glass beads, inhale the smell of porridge and meat stews being cooked in camp kitchen fires, hear the singing of village musicians. At such moments, Gilota seemed to dissolve, lose her personality, and merge with the colorful and polyphonic gathering of people. She went with the flow, smiling and enjoying moments of complete carefreeness. There is no personal responsibility in a crowd; on a holiday you can throw away thoughts about the past and not count on the future. In front of the modest stall of a herbalist who had reached the city from the distant southern mountains, she stood a little longer, then looked at the violinist musician with a tame monkey in a skirt, dancing to a folk dance tune.

A loud laugh somewhere ahead attracted her attention, but she was immediately distracted again, looking at the forged weather vanes. Gawking, I barely missed the organ grinder rushing ahead. Cursing, Gilota pulled back and a new stream of people picked her up and carried her somewhere.

- My child, give me a copper for food! - the old beggar woman wailed, trying to grab her by the elbow.

Only miraculously, Gilota evaded her strong hands, backed away and immediately fell into a liquid crowd, laughing and animatedly discussing something. From the push, a couple of onlookers parted without resistance.

- Look, look, stare! Everything is as if chosen! - shouted the merchant.

- Selected freaks! - one of the onlookers responded with laughter.

Discordant laughter rang out all around.

Gilota turned around curiously. On a vacant patch of fairgrounds stood a carriage with a large iron cage. A couple of guards were bored at the processing station, looking without any interest at the "goods" lined up in front of the cart, and they were slaves. A dozen, no more, but what kind. Gilota immediately understood why they had gathered a curious public around them. "Selected freaks." Everyone is on their knees, with downcast gazes. Dressed in dirty burlap. A blue-skinned and black-eyed northern barbarian, a cripple with elongated bones, a cripple with scabs on his skin that made him look like a living tree, a large-headed dwarf, a shaggy witcher with a brand on his cheek... Turning her gaze to him, Gilota froze. She blinked in surprise.

- A real thug with a stone head! Hit him in the face with even a shaft - he'll survive! — the trader did not let up.

He pulled the collar and dragged forward a large bald fellow, broad-shouldered, with muscles bulging under the skin and a narrow-minded monkey face, and Gilota, taking a quick glance, realized what was wrong with this "product." The kid was weak-minded. He smiled like a child and looked trustingly into the faces of the giggling onlookers.

Gilota looked again at the slave with the brand on his face.

"No, this can't be..."

- Oh, lady! - exclaimed the merchant. "It's rare that respectable ladies deign to pay attention to such exhibitions!"

Her strange attention to just one "product" did not escape him, because the merchant then dragged him by the collar.

- Here, for example, is an obedient little animal for exotic lovers! Have you ever seen something like this, huh?! A sorcerer from the capital itself! I'll give it for three coppers if anyone can point out where in the marketplace there is a second one like this! And if you don't find it, it's only three libras or eight dinars!

For every shouted phrase, he tugged at the slave's collar, and he awkwardly crawled behind him on his knees.

- Expensive! - one of the spectators said mockingly.

"The opportunity to show off your chain sorcerer to your friends is worth more than one piece of gold, really!" — the merchant responded in tone. - Look more closely, okay! — And with a kick in the ass he pushed the slave under the feet of the "venerable lady."

Gilota glanced at the escape route. And the merchant grabbed the man by the long, tangled hair, lifted his head and put his fingers in his mouth.

- The teeth are all intact! The bones are strong! Look, lady, look!

I wanted to turn around and leave. Gilota watched, fascinated. The noise of the fair faded away.

The slave was dirty, scary and humble, like a living corpse. He tolerated the demonstration of his teeth and the feeling of his muscles with indifference. When they let me go, he dropped his head, looking at the ground and hiding his face behind his matted hair. And even when the merchant tore at his rags, he did not move to cover himself. Gilota saw much more than was worth it.

"It can't be him."

She tried to convince herself that she was mistaken in attributing familiar features to the grimy and disfigured man. How many years had passed since that remembered man stood before her with a weapon in his hands, burning with righteous rage and ready to shed blood? Or... when she saw him for the first time and he was completely different?

Gilota bent down and called silently, with just her lips:

"Sir Thomas?"

Sometimes people miraculously recognize their own name, even when spoken in their thoughts.

He heard. He didn't raise his head, only his shoulders tensed. Gilota straightened up, suppressing the strong urge to touch his bowed head to make sure that he was a creature of flesh and blood and not a monstrous apparition. But she didn't move, she just closed her eyes, feeling the icy cold thickening somewhere inside.

"That's how it is. Sir Thomas, where is your trusty sword?.."

Once upon a time she changed his fate with one touch, and he became her mortal enemy. But they parted forever, they were separated by a whole all-consuming cycle, how many years have passed since then?

What does time do to the creation of her kind? It multiplies their strength. What can time do to a person? Just erase it into dust and dispel without a trace.

Gilota retreated, emerged from the crowd, and slowly walked away. She tried to tell herself that everything was useless. Everyone chooses their own path, and this man once stood at a crossroads and made the main decision in his life. He walked a path that he himself called "righteous" and "sacred." Now he kneels where his long journey ended.

No one has the right to deprive a person of this highest happiness - to collect the fruits of his own many years of labor.

She herself has not the slightest connection to this. It was another woman, her name was Oresia, she died long ago. Stop thinking about it, put it out of your head and go your own way, it's still long.

Gilota stopped in the middle of the crowd, as if she had encountered an invisible wall. The fair hummed and rumbled, and it seemed to her that she could still hear that roaring laughter with which the crowd greeted the man crawling on his knees in a slave collar.

She tried to tell herself that these were just human affairs and did not affect her life in any way.

Gilota herself did not notice, behind her heavy thoughts, how it happened, but she had already turned around and was pushing her elbows, making her way through the endless bustle back to the damned cart.

Part 3

Eighteen years ago.

The first to rush to the fortress was a messenger, bringing good news, and at the end of the moon the army of Ringern Raven appeared on the horizon. A line of horsemen, foot swordsmen, archers, masters of fire and gunpowder filled the highway. In the rearguard stretched an endless convoy. Oresia watched from the wall as the vanguard unfurled their banners as they approached the fortress. They swayed in the wind with black and red ribbons, and this sight resonated with warmth in my soul. Oresia made a bet and was not mistaken - of all the commanders of her late husband, Raven turned out to be exactly the one she needed now. He understood everything and doubted nothing.

In the evening, after the best warriors of Ringern Raven, led by their leader, paraded along the main street of the city, and the camp set up outside the city walls was covered by a cheerful wave of drunkenness and debauchery, Oresia already felt endlessly tired. But she endured while the maids dressed her in a formal outfit, which, because of the tight corset, seemed to her like a torture machine. Never mind, later she will dress as she pleases. Such a time will come.

While the servants hastily completed preparations for a sumptuous dinner, in the wide courtyard of the fortress a large retinue was examining the most valuable trophies, unloaded by the guards from the carts. The domains of the rebellious Baron Wyatt lay near the northern sea, and from his military campaigns his flotillas brought sparkling gold with particles of magical sand, dyed silk and patterned brocade, which were woven only with the help of special spells, to their native shores, precious stones that had never been found in the imperial lands, from the sight of which the empress's ladies-in-waiting were speechless in admiration, medicinal herbs and seasonings that grew so far away that when transported along land routes they became more expensive than some cities, magical powders from the bones of animals whose dwellings were no longer in this world. But why didn't all this magic help Baron Wyatt's sorcerers when it remained the only salvation?

That is why Oresia relied on reason before any spells.

She watched, standing on the high front steps, as countless chests and packages were opened. And I noticed how no new trophies were taken out of the next cart, but a man dressed in ceremonial attire was brought out. He wore a dark uniform embroidered with silver water ripples and a black cloak trimmed with fur. Long dark hair spilled over her shoulders. The guest indignantly twisted away from the hands of the guards who were trying to hold him by the elbows. Ringern Raven came up from behind, took him by the shoulder and began to insistently say something. The guest first shook his head, then turned around and looked at Orecia. The raven walked towards the stairs, tall, stately, dressed in a polished uniform, not covered with heavy armor and holding the hilt of a weapon on his belt, and the guest reached after him, clutching a sword in a simple sheath to his chest.

"Your Highness," Raven addressed from the foot of the stairs, and Oresia could hardly restrain a smile when the involuntary thought came to her mind that in bed he calls her something completely different. "Your faithful warriors, by the power of the sword, proved your right to own the northern land.

Orecia looked again at the one who could hardly be called a "guest". Young, probably no more than seventeen winters old. I recently received the right to wield my father's sword and command his people, and now I have to give everything up. The young man wearing the Wyatts' ancestral embroidery on his clothes was not a visitor, but a trophy like the jewels laid out for counting. Up close, it became clear that the clothes had become frayed on the long journey, and the main symbol of his family's defeat—his father's battle sword—he clutched to his chest with his shackled hands. But the young man's gaze was sharper than any sword.

The last living man of the Wyatt family.

The stubborn northern baron, once infinitely loyal to the Emperor, refused to recognize the suzerainty of his wife over himself, and even dared to call her a "usurper" and a "filthy witch." The capital had lost control of vast rich lands, and more than one ruler from distant provinces thought about joining the rebellion. The outskirts of the empire began to glow with the first fires of riots, ready to burst into violent, all-consuming flames. There was no other choice but to prove their power by force of arms. And now it's over. All that remained were smoldering coals, dying out under the soles of the soldiers' boots. The Wyatts were stronger than the others; the exhausting war, destroying resources and the lives of vassals, lasted a long time. But now it was all over.

Raven made a speech, the courtiers listened to the story of his military valor for the glory of the Empress. Orecia looked at Wyatt. He was handsome, like a forest spirit who had only briefly turned human. The eyes are light and completely devoid of the appropriate expression of humility. And then Raven finished his speech and retreated, letting the main military trophy pass ahead.

"I was told that if I did this, my people would be safe, you would not touch them or harm them," Wyatt said.

No proper treatment, no formalities. Orecia paused, but Wyatt was not embarrassed.

"The masters on whose orders they acted are responsible for the actions of the servants," said Oresia.

The prisoner nodded and, kneeling down, lowered his sword onto the last step of the stairs. The scabbard and hilt were wrapped with a thin strap, apparently to help the young oathbreaker restrain himself and not draw his weapon at the call of hot blood in order to sell his life at a higher price. He spoke quickly and loudly:

— I appeal to everyone who is able to hear this message and keep it in memory, and pass it on around the world. We, Thomas Wyatt, son of Osmond Wyatt, who have taken his sword and right, dominate the lands from the Black Strait to the mountains of Zellach. Take into account that our family served the Emperor and defended his lands, thereby gaining fame and recognition, until my father Osmond Wyatt, who in recent years went astray at the behest of the demons of reason and me, who sank after him. We, Thomas Wyatt, recognize ourselves as oathbreakers and ask for the greatest mercy that the hand of the Emperor can give us - to accept our weapons so that they can continue to serve for the good of the throne, and for us, oathbreakers, to be disposed of at the highest discretion for the sake of atonement for our grave crime...

For some reason, Oresia felt sad. The emperor is able to forgive those who break the oath, but this mercy has a high price - it can only be paid with blood. Oresia saw how her deceased husband gave forgiveness, and she herself has already performed this ritual more than once. The Emperor steps down the stairs to touch the bowed head, then steps back. A wave of his hand, the sword cuts through the air and the head, blown off his shoulders, rolls onto the sand, the Emperor says "you are forgiven and released."

She saw how, behind the bowed prisoner, Raven silently took his sword from its sheath.

Orecia took a step, another, and carefully placed her palm on Thomas Wyatt's bowed head. The insight that visited her at that moment was fleeting, but dazzling. It is unlikely that any of the courtiers had time to notice how her eyes under her half-lowered eyelashes were shrouded in darkness for a fraction of a moment.

She heard the calling melody of trumpets rousing the armies to attack, felt the downpour lashing her face with cold streams, saw what one of the many threads leading her to the future and intertwined with human choices and deeds.

Before her eyes, Thomas Wyatt received a crossbow bolt in the back, fell off a cliff into icy water, and the current of the river smashed his head against the rocks.

Having aged by tens of years, Thomas Wyatt closed his eyes and fell asleep forever on his wide deathbed, in the circle of those close to him.

Thomas Wyatt, not yet at all old, was writhing in convulsions on the blood-stained slabs of the throne room, slowly crumbling into dust under the influence of a deadly spell, and Orecia managed to recognize the pattern of her magic, but was immediately distracted, because Thomas Wyatt drank wine from the cup, his skin became getting dark quickly...

And then a black force tore him apart in the magic circle.

He died a dozen times in an instant, in those lines of fate that were not destined to materialize anyway, because Oresia saw that Raven had already raised his sword. She even saw how he lowered it with all his might, but could not cut the bone with the first blow, only blood sprayed out, and the prisoner fell face down with a wheeze. The raven struck again - the head rolled on the ground, the eyes wide open in amazement were covered with a black haze, and Oresia shuddered. Alas, all the courtiers saw this, and a dull, frightened whisper swept through the courtyard. Raven retreated, realizing what had happened.

The front steps were sprinkled with the blood of the sorcerer. Even though he didn't have time to realize his strength, but...

"Bad sign."

The obsession dissipated, Oresia again saw Raven raising his sword over his bowed head. All that was needed was one gesture. And Oresia raised her hand in warning.

"In our name, you are forgiven," she said.

* * *

Now

The slave did not look up as Gilota handed the coins to the merchant. He tied her new property's hands and gave the customer the free end of the rope, like a leash. But the acquisition did not try to resist, and it remained only a humiliating formality, like a collar and a brand.

Accepting the rope, Gilota made a barely noticeable awkward movement and scratched the merchant's palm with the sharp edge of the red stone in the ring. He didn't even seem to notice. And he won't notice in the future until the scratch turns red and the infection spreads through the veins, looking for a path to the heart. Gilota herself could not have explained convincingly what motive pushed her to this meanness, but at that moment it seemed to her that it would be fair.

After all, she was a simple woman making a living through cheap witchcraft, not a monarch deciding the fate of the world. It is not her responsibility to measure every action from all sides.

The slave trailed behind, holding on to her shoulder, and it was as if he was not there at all. Gilota tried to feel the presence of someone else's power nearby, albeit irrevocably sealed, but she saw only emptiness. People walking towards her retreated to miss her companion, and their glances flashed either apprehension or disgust, because they all noticed the mark marking the convicted sorcerer. How many of them could remember making way for this man to bow their heads respectfully as he passed by? No, that happened in another life.

Gilota led the man onto a familiar street, stopped in front of the door, and he stood a little behind, waiting for her to unlock the lock.

"This is my workshop, and, perhaps, my house too."

Under the soles of her boots, the old, dry steps creaked, and he walked barefoot, without a single rustle, like a ghost.

Another door opened into a dark corridor, where visitors usually took a long time to gather their courage to cross the threshold of the room that Gilota considered to be a work room. There was a wide table topped with a shiny copper burner, which among people of her profession had long replaced the fireplace with a cauldron, surrounded by alembics, retorts and flasks, some of which needed to be thoroughly washed. Among the scattered notes, instruments were lost that she forgot to return to their place. Shelves lined the walls, lined with books, boxes, packages and glass vessels, where something that had once been living beings or their parts floated in the muddy liquid.

"Did you read in those books that taught you witchcraft that time moves in a spiral, endlessly repeating itself in different variations?" - asked Gilota.

But only silence answered her. The guest, who was no longer a guest, was silent, without raising his gaze. Gilota thought about who he could be now. A trophy? But she just bought him, paying much less than she should for a thoroughbred stallion or a rare potion.

For the first time in a long time, she pulled back the curtains, letting bright daylight into the room.

Gilota felt that she would not like this, but she still turned around and carefully examined the man frozen at the door. He stood motionless, still bowing his head and lowering his bound hands. Worn sackcloth barely hid the body. Thin, with terribly protruding bones and rough scars, it is unlikely to be hardy enough for constant hard work. If it weren't for the rare mark, it wouldn't even be worth the coins she paid.

Walking around the slave, Gilota touched the clumsily applied dirty bandage on his forearm, and the man tensed, but did not try to remove his hand. This wound was fresh, and it was worth taking a closer look at it, but the rest... The marks could tell a long, sickening story about what was done to this person. The marks indicated that the man had been tortured. Not the way prisoners are interrogated in war, but slowly and professionally, so that it lasts a little longer than the victim can bear. Broken fingers. The crushed bones of the left hand had healed, probably due to the work of the prison doctor, but they remained so uneven that the hand no longer regained its previous mobility. Burns from ticks and hot knitting needles. Stripes of scars where the skin was cut off with thin straps. The nails, once torn off, remained rough and dark, like animal claws. And after all that had happened, they did not kill him, but treated him, branded him, deprived him of all his rights and sold him into slavery, like an exotic animal.

"I see that the path of a hero is difficult when he is deprived of the only thing that made him a hero—a real villain as an opponent."

They knew each other once. And in front of her was a man who now knew her better than hundreds of those who had been around before. Gilota was sure that he would definitely not bear this insult. At least he will raise his head and look at her, as happened before. After all, hatred is much closer to love than indifference.

-Where is your army now, victorious hero? Where did your allies go when the source of your common malice fell and vengeance was taken? Did it really turn out that not everything is so simple, but you tried again and found another culprit? They're on to the next nasty witch, and it turns out to be you.

She couldn't stand it and laughed evilly.

- Do you remember how you angrily shouted that I drowned the world in darkness, and for this I only had three years and one war? Well, you had ten years! Tell me, is this what the white light you worshiped looks like? Tell me, are you happy now?

There was no need to say that. But Gilota got excited and could no longer stop. Something dark, sticky, frozen from the past years, cracked and tore out, and words fell out like sharp stones. And the one to whom they were intended did not try to object, and this angered her even more.

- Can you hear me! - Gilota shouted. - You hear that, right?!

She took a step forward, swung and... stopped her hand. The man's head bowed, and only due to the difference in height did Gilota notice that he had closed his eyes.

For the first time, Gilota regretted that she had almost immediately stopped following the life of Thomas Wyatt when she was born again. There were too many threads in his destiny that no longer intersected with hers. He could become a commander, he could take the place of Raven, who he killed, he could regain his ancestral lands and become the king of a new northern state. She expected something like this from him. And she never thought that so soon he would stand before her as a disfigured shadow of his former self. Ten years ago he was just good enough to deserve a better fate.

"Look at me," Gilota ordered.

When the man finally looked up, his eyes were faded and empty, like glass. Gilota unwrapped the dirty bandage from his forearm and examined the deep laceration.

- What's wrong with your hand?

Silence.

Gilota looked at his face and wondered if he was even able to speak. Probably the previous owners didn't care about this. The man's tongue was in place, but if trouble happened to his throat... It's difficult, too difficult. You need to start with simple and obvious things.

— The wound looks bad. Follow me, I'll wash it and bandage it. We'll deal with the rest later.

She opened a small door, almost hidden behind a wide shelving unit. She turned around and froze in amazement.

The man stood at the edge of her desk, both hands clutching the lancet that had previously been lying among the papers. Having met her gaze, he took a step back, holding this pathetic weapon in front of him.

- Why, Thomas? - said Gilota. "This is a worn-out tool, it has been sharpened so many times that the blade has become thin." I cut paper with it. If you suddenly decide that...

She didn't have time to finish, because the man took another step back, and then, awkwardly turning his arms, plunged the blade into his throat.

Part 4

Now

Towards evening Isa came. Sitting in a chair with another book in her hands, Gilota heard the key turning in the lock, quick steps treading along the corridor, and the door of the tiny kitchen slamming. When Isa entered the laboratory, an apron was already tied over her black dress, and her hair was gathered in a scarf.

"Good evening, mother," she greeted in a ringing voice and made a short bow.

Gilota nodded absently.

- Are you sick, mother? - Isa asked, probably referring to the blood smeared on the floor.

Gilota nodded again and went back to reading. She devoted most of the day to this activity, the angular letters of the Horne language were already blurring before her eyes, flowing down from the page of the richly illustrated book. The stew was slowly brewing in my head. The sources either confirmed or refuted each other's statements, and not a single book brought clarity to the main question - how does it happen that a sorcerer becomes more helpless than a common person?

Gilote used to think she had a great library. She collected it for almost a century, and, feeling how everything was going down the damn dog's tail, she took out the most valuable volumes and hid them so that she could return to them again in a new cycle. A large sum of "lifting money" was also kept with the books, but now it was not about the coins that had long been spent on renting a house, but about knowledge. She formulated the question precisely, but could not find the answer anywhere. This happened to her a few times. Moreover, read on the fingers of one hand.

Somewhere in the background a busy bustle could be heard. Isa washed the flasks, wiped the accumulated dust from the table and shelves, swept the floor, scraped and washed the dried floorboards, using a dull knife to remove fresh blood from the cracks in the boards, which Gilota had not washed away during the day. She ran around the rooms with rags, tubs, and boiled instruments clanking on trays. Gilota has long learned not to pay attention to other people's affairs, even if books that are no longer needed are taken right from under her hands to be returned to the shelf. And with a jerk she returned from the yellowed pages to the real world, noticing an unwanted movement out of the corner of her eye.

"What's going on, Isa," said Gilota.

The girl froze, already placing her palm on the handle of the slightly open door.

"You yourself said, mother, that if you leave someone sick in the house, then it's up to me to look after him," Isa said offendedly, smoothing the hem of her apron, which had turned gray with time. "So I'm just wondering if I need to bring some water or wash something up."

She was interested, Gilota understood this very well. Without curiosity and the desire to stick your nose into someone else's business, it is difficult to become a student of a sorceress.

"I can handle this myself for the time being."

Isa nodded and stepped back from the door, but her face remained concerned.

"You have something to say, say it," said Gilota.

After hesitating, Isa took something wrapped in a rag from her apron pocket and showed it to her mentor. It was a burnt, blood-soaked slave collar. Gilota realized that she had completely forgotten about him, although she had a suitable excuse - when you are urgently saving someone's being, there is no time to think about trifles.

"It was lying under the table," Isa explained.

- Throw it into the oven and make sure it burns to ashes.

The girl hurried out of the room, returned only a quarter of an hour later, and when she opened the door, there was a burning smell from the corridor into the room. The girl had a full basket of the cheapest apples in her hands. After watching her, Gilota sighed heavily. She put the book down and rose from her chair.

- Okay, let's see what you learned this time.

Isa vacated one end of the table, sat down and laid out the first apple in front of her.

Four apples later, Gilota irritably shook off pieces of pulp from the hem of her dress and sighed heavier than before. I remembered with regret that I never got into the habit of hitting the student's fingers with a rod after each unsuccessful approach. The effectiveness of this method of education remained in doubt. But at least she would have enjoyed the process.

- Concentrate, girl, and get rid of everything unnecessary from your head, otherwise you will never advance beyond making raw materials for apple jam.

Isa concentrated, waved her hands and blew up the fifth apple. Gilota took the sixth one out of the basket, placed it in front of her and performed the necessary pass slowly so that the student could look at everything again. At first, nothing strange happened to the apple. Then it hissed and became covered in trembling bubbles, and a stream of steam rose upward. The peel burst and the boiling juice spilled over the countertop.

- Slow heating from the inside, see?

Isa nodded gloomily. And suddenly she asked:

- Mother, did someone really pay you to treat a slave?

Gilota chuckled. This means that everything was spinning in the girl's head all the time, not allowing her to take her work seriously.

"I'm afraid it's my own generosity." Because the slave is also mine, I bought him today at the fair.

If Gilota had admitted to her that this was not her first life, Isa could not have been more amazed. She really wanted to ask "why?", but she knew for sure that her mentor would not tell her about it. And she was apparently afraid to ask another question, although it was clearly visible in her wary gaze and sly smile, which she could not contain.

"I did not harm him," said Gilota. "And I didn't buy it to use it in a ritual." No, Isa. Never.

Isa turned pale and looked away.

- I don't understand, mother, because you...

"Ten years later, you yourself will already know the spells that are cast on human blood, and the rituals that require the most expensive sacrifice, because it is impossible to know the essence of phenomena without knowing this mechanism," Gilota interrupted her. "But you will never, never even think about doing this."

- Why? - Isa was surprised.

A simple answer "because it's impossible" would hardly have made her think.

- They will feel it. The abyss will stir, and everyone who can see will understand what happened. They will figure you out and start hunting you. This world lives according to laws written by horror and death, and it is not in the interests of those in the know to push it into the darkness, where it remained for many centuries, until the era of unspoken agreement came. One of the points of the agreement is no blood.

"It seemed to me, mother, that this is the goal of the initiates - to live long and learn to control ever-increasing power. Who could come up with such a thing - deliberately cutting off the most powerful branch of magic?

Gilota could have called them by name, but that didn't matter now.

- There is a creative power. And there is a corrupting one, and one that is fueled by blood, of precisely this nature. It is not the host who controls her, she herself quickly changes the sorcerer. Having crossed this line, you need to have the courage to face the consequences, but this is precisely the trap - the apostate does not have the strength to do this, his spirit is exhausted and requires new reinforcement. Once you take the path of killing for the sake of power, you cannot stop.

Gilota's sensitive hearing allowed him to discern a quiet rustling behind the wall of the laboratory. It creaked, knocked, creaked again, and then a muffled sigh was heard. What a bad time.

Isa sat, immersed in some gloomy thoughts.

"You have such a long way to go before you can make this choice, girl," Gilota told her. - Find out the arguments that you will put on invisible scales in order to understand what to do next. And now you can't even handle apples. We will have to return to this topic no earlier than in a couple of years. In the meantime, go, you can deal with the unfortunate fruits at home. Just clean up after yourself first.

When Isa left the house near the square, the lamplighters were already lighting lights on the streets, which were not safe even during the day. However, Gilota did not worry much about the girl - she was the daughter of a man whom most of the local tramps were afraid of, because they considered him the owner and even paid some kind of tribute from the wallets taken from late passers-by. And the owner of the beggars paid Gilota herself, knowing how important the help of a real witch can be in those matters where the law is the main enemy and threat to existence.

Having locked the door behind the girl, Gilota felt nervous. Now much depended on what decision she would make. Her own invisible scales could not give the correct answer. It was necessary to find very important words, but they were not found.

The room behind the office was small. The tight space accommodated everything that should have been at hand at the right time. Two lamps illuminated the mechanical table standing in the center of the room with an even yellow light. Once upon a time it was invented by one of those whom the girl Isa frivolously called initiates. The design, using levers, could raise or lower the tabletop to fix it at a convenient height. An incredibly expensive thing, the value of which not many will understand. Who cares about the convenience of surgical operations for those who still believe that all diseases come from unpleasant odors, and that profuse suppuration can wash away evil demons that feed on flesh from a wound?

The man lying on the table shuddered and immediately froze tensely. He looked a little better than before. A few hours ago, Gilota decided to cut off the rags from him, treat his wounds and wipe his body. The patient was still unconscious, which made the work slower. Now there were neat bandages on the arm and throat, which had already been soaked through with ointments and ichor. The decoction poured into the mouth worked, and the bluish pallor disappeared from the face.

The man was tied with belts by the arms and legs, because Gilota had no idea what other crazy act could be expected from him. They looked at each other tensely for a few moments.

- You missed the vein. Glory to the Abyss," said Gilota. - It was such a stupid thing to do! Do you think that at this very moment the afterlife would be easier? It seemed to me that after everything that happened, you hardly have anything to fear in this world.

The man turned away and stared at the ceiling, but as soon as Gilota let him out of sight to take freshly boiled bandages, a slight rustle was heard again, and the belt fastenings jingled.

- It won't work that way. If you jerk, you'll have to tighten the straps. I had to operate on this table on men who were stronger than you are now. What was it worth to the thug Tucker alone? They gutted him in the alley behind the Dancing Dead Inn. He struggled like a bear, but was only completely exhausted. Try something different, use your wits. You can gnaw your wrist like a fox. Or turn to your mind, if it is still with you - it will suddenly tell you something useful.

The movement stopped, but as Gilota approached to change the bandages, the man twisted his wrist in the belt loop and grabbed her arm.

- You are real...

The cold fingers clenched unexpectedly tightly, but Gilota didn't even think about breaking free and just stared at the man in amazement, trying to figure out if she had heard something wrong. She saw the movement of the caked lips, but the voice was no louder than the rustle of book pages. And then the man made a strange sound, as if he wanted to cough, but he restrained himself and let her go.

"What do you... want..." he muttered barely audibly and turned away, barely catching his breath.

- First of all, you need to tell me what happened.

Gilota went into the room and returned with a glass of water, but the patient twitched in fear just by looking at him.

- What... there...

- You need to drink.

He choked and coughed dryly. Gilota rushed to the table, but the man sharply shook his head, dodging the touches. And when she tried to support the back of his head and brought the glass to her mouth, she pressed her lips tightly together.

"Drink, it will make you feel better, come on, just a couple of sips," she admonished him, like a capricious child, then backed down.

Gilota remembered her mother telling her that witchcraft always leads men to misfortune. They are not created for this fate, and if someone is born with the makings of a sorcerer, then he should not expect a happy life and an easy death. Perhaps now it didn't sound as funny as before.

When she put the glass away and returned to change the damaged bandages, the man was already lying with his eyes closed and did not move anymore. She leaned over his face, placing her palm on his forehead, trying to catch the slightest vibration of power, but there was nothing there. It was as if she was looking into an empty shell. There was not a single sign that this man had once been able to cut down an entire squad of guardsmen, relying on a single hastily cast magical shield, and when he attacked, the power splashed out of him like a tidal wave, because he had never fully learned to hold she is in check. How careless it is to think more about the defeat of the enemy than about your own safety. But power, even if handled carelessly, cannot completely leave the owner. If it is not here, it means that someone else took it and is using it. So, they allowed her to be taken away.

- What have you done? - said Gilota.

The man slowly shook his head.

* * *

The wound on the hand was bad, and no one took care of its cleanliness in time. Gilota didn't understand what could hit her like that, but judging by the direction of the explosion, the man shielded his head from this object.

A decade and a half ago, she could not imagine the possibility of young Sir Thomas Wyatt wearing a slave collar and only covering his head when he was beaten. Apart from old, long-whitened scars, there were no traces on his knuckles, which means he didn't resist.

- You know, sometimes this strange thought came to me - what if I'm wrong? What if you are right, and I don't see the obvious? You may be surprised - yes, I was overcome by doubts. Ringern told me, when the fire of hatred began to flare up again in the north, that I treated you too softly, pardoning you, and even allowing you to escape. In his opinion, if I didn't want murder, then it was worth locking you in the tower forever. Or deprive him of his title, flog him in public, like a presumptuous lackey, and send him to colonies on some distant islands.

Gilota tightened the knot on the new bandage.

- If you were surprised, the thought "which colonies?" flashed through your head, I will clarify for you that they are the same ones that you lost in the first year after the overthrow of tyranny. The same ones that supplied resources to the lands stricken by long-term drought from the continental coast to the Ring of Fire, are now empty and inhabited only by small, half-starved tribes of savages, who are captured by traders and sold for coppers into slavery in iron mines and coal mines. Perhaps you have met such people in recent years. And now it seems to me that Ringern was monstrously right. Five dozen marks that will heal in a couple of years, and you, educated and modest, are already in charge of some plantation, amassing a fortune and acquiring an accommodating local wife, or maybe three at once. You would, of course, never be allowed to return to the continent, but is that a reason for sadness? If Ringern were alive, he would laugh like a demoniac.

- Yes, and you... are not far behind...

Gilota, who was collecting damaged bandages for washing, looked at the man with slight surprise.

- You lie... and mock... When... will you get down to business?.. Why do you... need me?..

- To mock.

The man twitched, making the same dull sound, but now his chapped lips stretched, and Gilota guessed that it was a grin the last time as well.

"We both know..." he said very hoarsely and again coughed so much that Gilote had to wait a while to find out what she knew about, because the man again dodged the glass of water.

"You lied... to the girl," he finally spoke. Now the voice was hoarse. It was as if an instrument that had not been used for a long time had completely broken down and now did not want to serve its owner.

"You can do a lot to a person... And there's so much blood on your hands... Are you frowning?.. Only the dead... needn't be afraid of you... But I... didn't let you die... You're holding out... pleasure..."

In fact, Gilota was frowning because it was difficult to understand the rustling and interrupted speech. But something told her that explaining such trifles to a person determined to die was a futile undertaking. So she just threw up her hands.

"Forgive me, I'm too angry and I'll try to shorten my tongue in the future."

She understood that she could not say anything that the man himself had not tormented himself with in recent years, whatever he thought about, whatever he regretted, while there was still strength left for regret and grief. He had a lot of time to plunge circle after circle into his personal hell. But for some reason it was too difficult to stop myself. What is this? An inescapable resentment at what her clearly constructed world has become?

The man coughed and squeezed out with difficulty:

"You're not evil... you're evil."

Gilota even smiled. A mind capable of composing a play on words in such a state cannot yet be considered lost in the Abyss.

"Drink," she said, again offering the glass and placing her hand under the back of his head.

- What is this.

- You need to drink.

The man turned away.

"What is this," he repeated stubbornly.

"Datura," answered Gilota, feeling that all this was beginning to bother her. "You'll fall asleep for a while, it's okay."

- What... are you doing... Orecia.

There was clearly desperation in his voice.

"That's not my name, I was never really called that," said Gilota and added softly: "I won't do anything bad, I'll just ease your suffering." Don't be afraid, Thomas.

- So... that's not... my name anymore.

"Okay, and I won't be there until the time comes," Gilota agreed easily. "Be that as it may, you must drink what they give you." Otherwise, you will have to pour in the swill by force. Fear not, brave knight. After all, you were once not afraid of anything, or did it just seem that way to me?

The man went limp and closed his eyes.

- I... am a cowardly dog and...

Gilota didn't let him finish; she forced him to unclench his jaw and poured the sleepy broth into his mouth.

- That's all.

"That's it..." the man echoed.

His gaze wandered around the room, watching how Gilota took the bandages to be washed, straightened the soft mat on the table, placed a small pillow at the head, brought a dozen red wax candles, stones in velvet bags, a long knife... The man's eyes became dull, his body relaxed. Gilota reached out and closed his eyelids.

Not a sound was heard from the street, and the old house slept, plunged into darkness. But the people lying in their beds, until recently quiet and peaceful, as if sensing something, groaned in their sleep when Gilota closed the magic circle, and a feeling of danger spread across the world, invisible to the ordinary eye.

Gilota climbed onto the table and sat down, straddling the man's hips. She ran the tip of the knife along her left palm, stretched, pressing herself closely to the body, placed her bleeding hand on the man's forehead and uttered an order in a language that had been used for hundreds of years only on such bad nights.

The man's eyes widened, filled with inky darkness.

* * *

The sun was still seeing its last dream over the distant horizon when there was a persistent knock on the door of Erevard Eagle Prim's town house. The sleepy servant, promising all sorts of punishments to the dissolute guest, opened the door, shone a lantern and stepped back, quickly muttering apologies. Behind the threshold stood a girl in a black cloak with a hood and holding a package in her hands. The servant knew her too well, she was a witch with whom the owner for some reason got confused.

"I need your master," said the girl.

Raised as if on alarm, the cook began to prepare the master's brew to raise her spirits, the maids lit candles in the small living room.

At the invitation of the footman, Gilota sat down in a carved chair with a high back and placed a bundle on her lap. With displeasure, she examined the interior of the living room, replete with patterned fabrics, curlicues, and shiny trinkets. The only thing that didn't fit here at all was a large painting in an overly ornate frame. However, this was exactly what she expected to see. Against the background of a dark stormy sky, the polished armor of the three warriors shone like bright pearls. The faces are smooth, much smoother than they were in life, untouched by fatigue, scars, and the first signs of old age. Plates with names were inlaid into the frame, the letters of which could not be seen from the chair. It didn't matter, because Gilota could name them from memory.

"Sir Ernald Big Ash, Knight of the Dead Land." The artist seemed to have forgotten that the hero lost his right eye and bore a dozen scars on his face.

"Sir Rohyr Colette, bearer of the sword called Sorrow." The current ruler of the imperial lands, or rather, what is left of them. There's not much left.

"Sir Thomas Wyatt, Master of the Wind." The look from the painting was such that it seemed to Gilote that the portrait would now open its mouth and begin to insult her with the last words.

- You?.. Sorry, dark lady, I wasn't expecting you so early.

The owner of the house appeared in the living room, shaggy from sleep, wrapped in a thick robe. A look in which he dared to appear to very few people. Gilota had seen him in worse condition.

- Good health to you, sir.

Erevard saw the package in her hands, became nervous and quickly sat down in the chair opposite.

- So soon! Sorry, I didn't know!

- I came early. It's better when time remains in reserve, rather than running away at the last moment. You will receive one part with the first rays of dawn," said Gilota. - The second one is at midnight. Now I will stay here and help you for the first time. The second one you have to do everything yourself.

Hereward nodded quickly. Gilota clutched the package tighter so that he would not notice how her fingers were trembling. She was so exhausted that she collapsed into bed and did not wake up until the next dawn.

And she even felt sorry for the old man opposite in her own way. He died very slowly. Life was leaking out of him in tiny drops, and what she held in her hands could only delay the inevitable for a short while. By her standards - for moments. For the old man, it was a couple of years - an eternity, incalculable wealth. And he gave up his entire wealth to sit now and wait for the right moments.

— Are you attracted by the picture, dark lady? asked Hereward.
He was nervous and clearly wanted a distraction.

- A very talented creation. Who was the artist?

"His name was Nickel, but, unfortunately, he has already left us.
Gilota pretended that this upset her.

"And who are these two men on both hands of our ruler?"
Erevard grinned good-naturedly.

- Frankly, I am surprised that you recognized the ruler, but the rest - alas... These three noble knights made the world what it is now. They returned light to the lands of the Empire.

"But it's hard not to know the face of the ruler." I even saw him once when I was in the capital. On the square, he addressed the people. His speech made me tear up with emotion. But I have never seen these noble warriors.

"It's not surprising, because they are no longer with us," Erevard said and looked at the picture again with sincere sadness in his eyes. - These are the noblest of people. Sir Ash and Sir Wyatt.

-What happened to them?

- Don't you know? Not only did you not see them, but you also didn't hear their names?

Gilota shrugged guiltily.

"When it all happened, I was sixteen, and I lived in the wilderness. My husband did not bring me news from the city.

— Did you have a husband? — the old man was amazed and immediately raised his hands in an apologetic gesture: "Sorry, I shouldn't have asked you such questions, dark lady."

Gilota just smiled tightly. Of course, she had a husband in this life. When she was transported, devastated after a mortal battle, she had no strength left in her to fight off this "husband." After all, he, of course, called her his wife and dragged her into his house. She began to live with him in the forest. Just where Oresia drove rotten people like her husband - into a remote thicket, from where they were afraid to even get out onto the highway to get their living. But they weren't afraid for very long. After the change of power, the road bandits, who now had no one to diligently catch and put on stakes along the highways, perked up and came into force again. It's a pity that she had to wait a whole six months to burn the whole gang alive.

- So what happened to them?

- Sir Ash died from the plague in the southern lands. That year, when she almost reached the Ring of Fire, but Sir Ash did not want to flee, he maintained order among the sick and those still healthy until the last. Dying, he still gave out instructions. Sir Wyatt went as a negotiator to Anhalli, but the Atarians tracked down his squad and killed almost everyone, only one managed to survive. Sir Wyatt was driven to the river and wounded by a crossbow bolt. He fell into the water and died among the stones.

"I hope the survivor managed to return the body to the capital?"

- No, unfortunately for us. Our hero lies in a foreign land, and he probably doesn't even have a gravestone. Only his squire managed to survive; the poor boy survived captivity among the Atarians, was severely maimed and irreparably damaged in his mind.

"Monstrous," said Gilota quite sincerely.

"The best of us leave early," said the old man.

- What about the young man?

- Sorry?..

Gilota glanced briefly at her watch. There was only time for one question and answer.

- Sir Wyatt's squire. Is he still alive?

"He's alive, but I said, the poor fellow is too disfigured." He is being kept locked up somewhere.

Gilota rose, and the folds of her clothing straightened out with a serpentine rustle.

- What is time? — Erevard was alarmed.

She nodded.

- Let's prepare you to take the drug.

Part 5

Gilota returned home already in the growing light of day. She looked into a ready-made clothing store and somehow, spreading her arms and rising on tiptoe, explained to the merchant what size to choose for her. It is unlikely that exact measurements were important when a person simply had no other clothes. Of all the shirts and pants laid out on the counter, I chose those with stronger fabric and more secure seams. The most expensive one here was a cloak with a deep hood so that you could cover your face.

A loud and colorful fair day rolled through the city streets. Gilota felt the fatigue buzzing in her head more and more insistently. Making her way through the crowd and holding the bundle of purchases so that the nimble thieves would not snatch it from her hands, she could no longer make out the swirl of goods and the faces of passers-by, but she suddenly caught the scent, the sour smell of tanning, from the general confusion of aromas and stench, and slowed down in front of the stall tanner. There were dozens of collars lying on a wide counter. Simple leather strips, both embroidered with metal plaques, and with short blunt spikes on the inside, and hung with bells and beads. The latter even looked somewhat festive, and Gilota suppressed an inappropriate laugh. If only she could get herself a big, curly poodle. It's not at all like bringing a sick and perhaps even mentally deranged man into the house. However, no "maybes". Gilota involuntarily remembered the prickly fear in the moment when someone else's blood was pouring into her hands, and she was trying to tear off the slave collar that was preventing her from getting to the wound...

The good mood disappeared like incense smoke from the wind, and fatigue fell on my shoulders with renewed vigor. I barely had enough strength to get home.

On the stairs, Gilota leaned on the railing only once - from this effort, her forearm under the tight bandage burned with acute pain.

This was an impressive hint that the hand would now have to be protected for a while. But she had no other way out to save someone else's life, which means she had nothing to regret.

The man was still fast asleep, and his face looked tense in his sleep. Gilota placed the packages of shopping on the edge of the table. She put her palm to the sleeping man's forehead. The eyelids fluttered.

"Hey," Gilota called quietly.

But he didn't wake up. So she has a little more time for herself.

My head felt empty and heavy. She is very tired. Although, what's strange about this? She herself decided to help her "neighbor." She unwrapped the bandage to make sure that the piece of someone else's wound on her hand looked much better than the day before. The terrible inflammation subsided. Gilota sat down at the table. Just take a couple of minutes to catch your breath.

- You know, the moment I saw you... It was like I was pricked by a needle. And then everything was haunted by a certain vague insight. I suffered for a long time, trying to figure out what was stuck in my thoughts, like a splinter, but now it is clear, because there is only one question: why are you alive now? There is no stupider way to get rid of a person - to put him up on the market...

Gilota couldn't help but grin, because she herself had just realized what this could really mean:

- Only if that was not the goal - to be seen. Oh, how simple it is. Bait for fools. Some last fool who will be in the right place at the right time and will be so selfless that he will not pass by...

She touched the man's hand, but he did not react to the touch.

- What does this mean, huh? - Gilota asked.

It seemed to her that now he was definitely faking it. No, he was actually still unconscious.

- Amazing, Sir Thomas. It's amazing how sometimes you can find out interesting news. Even if you don't want it at all.

Of course, he didn't answer her, and Gilota felt too tired.

"There is time. If trouble hasn't happened yet, it can wait at least a couple of minutes," she told herself, closing her eyes.

* * *

Twelve years ago

- What do you want?

"I want to kill her," replied Thomas Wyatt.

Rogier Colette noticed that there was no strong emotion in his voice. A young man can be forgiven for his heated words and deeds, but no, this one was so calm that he inspired respect. Rohyr raised his eyebrows, smiled fatherly and clarified:

- Do you need revenge?

"I want to kill this slut. Take her life the way her dogs took everything from me, thought Thomas Wyatt.

"That's what brought me to you," he said out loud.

"I guessed where you were trying to get," Rogier Colette nodded.

Thomas had been looking for these people since the end of spring and had become desperate.

The day before this fateful meeting, the banks of the Ela River were covered with the first, still thin ice. After getting out of the forest, Thomas discovered that the old bridge no longer existed. He stood for a long time among the rubble, wrapped in multi-layered rags and looking at the dark water running in the riverbed. With each breath, clouds of steam rose into the chilly air.

Somewhere far from here, the river rushed among the rocks and stones to meet the waters of the Black Strait, the land that had belonged to his family since ancient times. But here it became an insurmountable obstacle. Climbing into icy water is suicide. He won't be able to dry his clothes by the fire in a way that will keep him warm. And he has no way to the nearest crossing. It is here, near the collapsed bridge, that the lands were abandoned by people many years ago because of some curse that ordinary villagers believed in. Upstream along the banks were scattered dozens of villages, fisheries, farmsteads, and small towns. For many months in a row, guard detachments capture all the tramps that pass through their land. In every tiny village, residents are warned about the fugitive criminal, and the amount of the imperial reward for his skin is such as not to leave the slightest doubt. Raven took into account all the ways that the escaped prisoner could use. If you get too close to human habitation, he will be captured. Wyatt knew about it, but couldn't think of anything. Too tired.

The hungry season brought fierce packs of predators to hunt, and even a short nap in the forest became unsafe. Having not seen sleep for several days, Wyatt simply walked along the shore, and walked, and walked... When armed people blocked his way in the wilderness, and the path to retreat was cut off, Thomas could no longer even think that this was the end of the road. I decided that I would at least take more attackers with me. But they did not come for his death.

"And I will not hide that such an ally would be very valuable to me in these times."

Thomas tried to keep an indifferent expression on his face. Oh, of course! They were hiding in the windswept ruins of some ancient fortress, and, as far as he could judge, the rebel noble's current garrison was quite small. Every fighter should be important to such a poor army.

And this is all that remains of Sir Osmond Wyatt's allies... Nothing. The heir would only like to get to his native land. He knows what kind of people to lead.

- But, there is always a "but", Sir Wyatt. How long were you at court? You see, I have the right to somewhat doubt the loyalty of a possible comrade-in-arms if he has already betrayed his patron once.

Here he could not stand it - he angrily squeezed the armrests of the chair.

"The only patron of my family was the Emperor, and I did not betray him, and if you want to say otherwise, then I will consider it an attack on my honor." My family was destroyed, I was brought to the capital as a trophy. I was "at court" exactly as long as it took to organize the escape, and I didn't stay a single day.

Thomas saw that Rogier Colette was in no hurry to trust him, but he was ready to endure this, for the time being. He himself cannot cope with the great goal. And without the support of the latter, Wyatt and Sir Colette will face defeat, although he doesn't think about it yet. Or maybe, on the contrary, I thought too often.

"I did not want to offend you and your family." We were friends with your father. You speak the right words, young Wyatt, and I wish I could believe them. Here you are surrounded by people who can understand your desire. But let us understand your actions too. I would like to hear the story of how you escaped from the imperial stronghold.

"I had Orecia's trust," Thomas replied. - And weapons against her.

Rogier Colette looked him up and down with a long, unreadable gaze. He thought slowly and thoroughly, no doubt weighing many options.

"And an unlimited supply of luck, I guess?"

- No. I didn't rely on her. I relied only on my weapon.

Sir Colette pursed his lips, then made the following move:

- Just your sword? I dare say my people did not speak highly of its quality.

Thomas smiled.

"This sword is a jagged piece of iron, I got it on the road to shoo away wild animals, and I couldn't even get hold of a suitable shield." But my weapon is always with me, it is not made of metal, and it cannot be taken away from me. And I am ready to put it at your service.

Rogier Colette again plunged into thought, then asked the main question:

-What do you want in return? What is the price for your allyship?

- Not great. There are only two heads - the ones I have to take myself. Orecia and Raven.

The leader of the tiny army chuckled dryly.

"I'm not sure you have the strength to carry away such a reward."

This was already starting to seriously irritate me.

"There's always a choice," Thomas said. "I can fight shoulder to shoulder with you." I can go away and gather my own loyal people. I think the most fruitful solution would be to join forces.

Still appraising him with his eyes, Sir Colette corrected:

"We won't be able to let you go; no matter the outcome, you'll have to stay in the camp." You've seen too much, Sir Wyatt. I hope you understand this yourself.

"That's why I propose an alliance." Otherwise, I would have gotten up and left in spite of everything, and you have nothing to stop me.

Colette frowned.

"I have to understand what I'm dealing with before I make an alliance."

Thomas held out his hand. The air above his fingers swayed, swirling into a tiny but undeniably ferocious vortex.

"I am skilled in witchcraft," said Thomas.

- You are the same as Orecia.

- No. Otherwise I would not have sought a meeting with you. Or you would already be dead.

"Is this the weapon that terrified the capital's guards and helped you make this unthinkable escape?" - Colette asked gloomily.

- Not really. I told you, I had two keys - Orecia trusted me. Now I'll take it with something else," Thomas said.

And as he uttered these words, he felt confident - he thought he was telling the truth.

Only much later did he realize that Orecia did not trust anyone. Thomas was wrong that time. And he made a mistake twice, trusting Rogier Colette.

* * *

Now

It seemed to him that this is what death should look like. He no longer had flesh. The usual sensations of heaviness and pain were cut off from the consciousness suspended in emptiness. This... no, he knew that the offensive nickname no longer concerned him, that he was a man and he had a name, but now it didn't matter, because everything that was left of this man slowly swayed on the soft warm waves, throwing away what had been eaten away by fears and deprivation of the body.

The man shuddered and the obsession dissipated.

The body stretched out to its full height lay on something flat, hard, dry... He opened his eyes, and returning to the living world turned out to be painful, like falling from heaven into the Abyss. Waking up in a stone bag or cage, he imagined that nothing in the world could no longer cause him suffering - he had survived everything. And once again I was wrong. Overhead, instead of an iron grille, there were darkened ceiling beams, and the yellow light of candles swayed on them. There was also a window in the room, but it was too narrow, like in a dungeon. But in the casemate the prisoner is given greater freedom of movement than he now has. The belts did not press, but held tightly. There was no point in counting on anything else, since they didn't deal with him right away. And they didn't allow themselves to be killed, they immediately carefully treated them, not sparing their own strength.

The witch needs him for some reason. This means that she will not allow the prisoner to try to die again before she really takes care of him. For everything he did for the witch, there will be no quick retribution. Maybe she will heal him like this more than once, so that he can last longer, she will have enough strength. This is Oresia. In any case, the creature that was her for some time. It was naive to believe that with this stupid attempt to pierce one's throat one could escape from her. And even here she flattered him - she decided that he had the courage to try again. The only hope is that she will get bored with him. It doesn't take much to scare him now, and he has completely forgotten how to endure pain with dignity. Its safety margin ended many years ago. To a sophisticated mind it must seem extremely boring entertainment.

The man moved carefully. He raised his head, examining himself... and froze, meeting the attentive gaze of dark eyes. The witch sat very close and smiled. This means that he woke up, and she simply looked at him, without betraying her presence. Was she watching what he would do, would he try to free himself? A nervous shiver ran through his skin, he could not contain it.

The witch stood up, stretched out her hand and removed the sticky hair from his wet forehead.

- Good morning. You felt it, right? I think it's gotten a lot better.

Better - what? The situation he now finds himself in?

In recent years, he had increasingly less control over his body, and it instinctively shuddered at sharp sounds and other people's movements, tried to shrink, tensed in anticipation of something bad, even from the gentle touches of women's hands. Although, is this really a woman? And if he had to fear anything else in this world, it was those hands. The man clenched his teeth.

"It's nothing, nothing, just repeat it out loud: I'm a cowardly dog, I'm scared, I'm very afraid that it will hurt again..." an invisible voice whispered in his ear.

The witch looked into his eyes and gently forced him to tilt his head towards the light.

- How do you feel? - she asked, looking into his eyes with concern.

And that was the worst thing. Imagine, even if just for a moment, that she actually genuinely cared about him. Because he is weak enough to believe it.

- Why do you need me? - he said and was amazed at how strong his voice was.

The witch smiled, softly and even a little guiltily.

"It seemed to me that we should postpone such a conversation if you are not feeling too well."

- What will you do to me? - he said.

She smiled wider. A tightly braided black braid lay on her shoulder, her face was very young, untouched by fatigue and wrinkles. She looked as if their first meeting had happened just yesterday. Even when the witch leaned over him so that their faces were too close, not a single flaw could be noticed. And this, probably, was the most important sign of her inhuman nature. A young and beautiful girl who will remain like this forever, no matter what you do to her.

- Take a deep breath, exhale slowly. "You look like you're going to have a stroke right now," said the witch.

The man remembered the feeling when the blade entered living flesh, and warm blood poured down his hand. It is impossible to survive after this; he himself closed the eyelids of the murdered woman. But then, when he returned to pick up the body and bury it, he was gone. The witch simply disappeared. He should have at least been wary, but he still believed that fate was favorable to him.

- What will you do to me? - he repeated stubbornly.

The witch pulled away and looked at him with a long, thoughtful look.

"It depends only on you now," she finally answered.

Part 6

Through the narrow window, Gilota looked out over the square. The sun rose above the roofs of the houses, the shadow of the empty pedestal shrank and crawled to the foot, where three tramps were located. The two slept with their heads down and their tattered jackets wrapped tightly around them. And the third looked directly at Gilota. So, at least, it seemed to her at first. Then she realized that this could not be, it was precisely her that he did not see in the shadows behind the curtain and glass, which had not been washed for many years. But he looked precisely at the windows of her rooms.

When a quiet creaking sound was heard in the silence, Gilota turned around sharply. The man immediately lowered his hand, feeling the belt on his wrist.

"If you're hoping that I'll be able to tell you something important, then you're in vain," he said. - All the secrets that I could know have lost any value over the years.

- I want to know what happened to you.

Pursing his lips, the man was thinking about something. Then he grinned wryly, although his facial expression remained somehow pitiful:

- But I knew that you were alive. All this time. At first I only suspected, but then... The darkness is indestructible, right?

"Like shadows on a sunny day," answered Gilota.

There was an unpleasant tingling sensation inside. Did you know then? But how did he manage to find out and from whom? No, that's nonsense. But still...

- Did you really hope that we would meet again?

The man didn't answer. He was waiting for something, and his rapid breathing betrayed his fear. But the look in the sunken eyes was surprisingly clear, much more meaningful than the night before. Gilota listened to herself, to the pain of others that the hastily performed ritual over the dying man brought her. She touched the thread stretched over the Abyss and could not contain her amazement. The invisible fiber stretched. And what is there on the other side?.. No, I can't feel it yet. Only a phantom wound on the arm under a tight bandage responded with aching pain and began to ooze not imaginary, but living ichor. Shouldn't have touched it. Blood magic affects both connected objects, and is always not as safe as we would like. Everything that is required will have to be learned in words.

"You have nothing to worry about now," she said. - As you can see, we have already met, but the world has not collapsed, and the sun still rises in the east. Anyone who crosses the threshold of my house is safe. They usually say that everyone judges by himself, but somehow I can't imagine you dealing with the weak and downtrodden. Despite what you may think, I'm not that dangerous.

Something flashed in his eyes, a glimpse of what was there before. The burnt cheek had long since healed, but half of the face remained somehow irregular, and Gilota could not say exactly what kind of strange expression slipped across that face and disappeared again.

- That's how it is... So, it's me who is dangerous? - he asked and desperately tugged at the straps. "Don't say that this is out of great concern for me."

Gilota allowed herself to smile:

"This is out of great concern that you don't sleepily stick yourself with another sharp object that comes to hand." I didn't give eight dinars just to get a fresh dead body.

The verbal blow aimed at pride was again in vain.

"It's better to be sure that you won't do anything stupid again," Gilota added more softly, leaning over him. - In the meantime, it's important for me to know - what happened to you? Who did it?

The man swallowed hard and spoke quickly and abruptly:

- I feel your breath. You are alive. She came for me. I thought I was wrong. I thought it was a mess. But you're real. And still - a ghost.

Can't you be destroyed? I saw you die. But the body... when I came back to pick it up, you were already gone. There was nowhere. Asked questions to others. They decided that something was wrong with me. Then I realized - I only thought I killed you. And you haven't played this game. You left. We're just boring you. I imagined later that you would remember and come for me. When you want to have fun. Was sure. I wasn't even surprised when you stood and looked at me. Yes, I'm a coward, I was scared. I thought what you would do to me. And you...

The man paused and coughed dryly. He was already shaking as if with a fever. Gilota looked into his whitened face, and therefore noticed the moment at which the mask of madness cracked. She reached out her hand to touch the bandage on her throat, but the man flinched and tried to move away. He breathed heavily through clenched teeth and gazed into her eyes. Sighing, she shook her head.

"I think I figured out how you survived," she said. - So you got out, huh? They left us alive at first because they believed in cooperation. They started with the left hand and did not mutilate the right, because there was still a chance to order you to take up arms. But it began to seem to them that your sanity was leaving you over time. And they believed you again, decided that now you are helpless and safe? Amazing. Previously, I remember, you didn't know how to pretend at all. But in my house it's no longer worth it. You are doing something very stupid again.

Of course, he did not want to understand her. Gilota realized with surprise that she was completely unpleasant that this man was afraid of her. We should have taken a different route. She grabbed his clenched fist and pulled, forcing him to place his hand under the tabletop.

- Unclench your fingers, don't be stubborn.

It seems that he discovered what she was trying to show him, because amazement immediately showed on his haggard face.

- What...

"I'm trying to make you calm down and answer my questions." It is important to know one thing about this table: the poor fellow with a ripped open belly or crushed bones is completely devoid of intelligence. In horror and panic, a person will struggle like crazy, and will never, ever stop to carefully examine his situation. So a drowning person destroys himself, floundering and swallowing water.

The man tried to pull his hand away. Gilota gently pressed his fingers lying on the mechanism, and something clicked loudly under the tabletop. The belt hung loosely and slipped off my wrist.

- Stop thinking as if the worst thing is going to happen. You're missing out on a lot. Regarding the situation in which you find yourself, one thing is important for both of us - this is not an accident. You were specially put up for sale. Maybe they were going to see who would rush to help. You have been used before, and they are using you now, as bait. Does Sir Thomas Wyatt have friends left who escaped a sad fate? If so, then when the trap slams shut, your skin will be completely devalued, and more worthy people will die, whom you probably do not wish to die.

He wanted to say something, but he just pursed his lips.

"I'm not trying to extract anything valuable from you," Gilota said. "I just need you to remain reasonable in case of sudden danger." We have a lot to talk about.

Muffled by the closed door, a hasty knock echoed through the house, causing the man to flinch. Gilota also tensed, and only after a few moments she felt that everything was okay, it was just Isa. She warned of her arrival before unlocking the door with the key given to her.

Gilota quickly wrapped the man's almost healed hand with a clean rag and shifted the bundles of purchases to the edge of the table.

"You have at least half an hour until I receive the student and send her out." First, get dressed. But you can, of course, try to escape through the window or bang your head against the wall. I'll just try to trust you, and hope that you're still smart enough not to do something like that.

The man smiled mirthlessly.

* * *

Isa looked unusually quiet and pale. She had already placed a rag bundle of fresh apples on the table and dragged a basket with provisions for the coming week into the pantry. When Gilota entered the large room, the girl was just tying her apron, habitually looking around in search of possible disorder.

"Mother, something is wrong with your slave," she said without any preamble.

- Is that so?

"I was told to tell you that they showed interest in your property." Two well-dressed gentlemen were asking in the square near the Bronze Town Hall where they could find a merchant of freaks, but he died tonight from something. They say that a chest demon strangled him. And the gentlemen kept asking him about the product, about the witcher with the mark. Eddrick was chatting with them, and it seemed to him that someone's groom hovering nearby was also listening to the conversation, although he didn't show it. He and Hugo wanted to intercept a lackey somewhere in a narrow alley, but he didn't leave them like a lackey, he turned out to be cunning.

Gilota was not even surprised that her patron knew which merchant sold her the slave. In a world of swindlers and dodgers hunting for other people's wallets, information about all familiar faces spreads quickly.

"Father says that if something bad doesn't happen." You should assign someone for safety.

- One of your people or what? - Gilota grinned. - And what will he do in case of real danger - die first? No, I can handle it myself. Let's get to work.

Isa still looked too tense, but she fried three apples according to the rules before there was a crash from the side room, as if something heavy had rolled across the floor, and the fourth apple scattered into smoking pieces. The girl stood up and looked at Gilota with alarm.

"Sit," she ordered.

The fifth apple repeated the fate of the fourth.

"A little better than it was," Gilota sighed heavily.

The girl sat without looking up.

- Try again.

It was clear how hard she was trying, but... Of the next five apples, only two were baked without failure. Isa kept looking warily at the door of the small room, and this brought down her entire mood. And there, as luck would have it, fuss, creaks and blows were heard.

Finally, the door swung open sharply, and the man swayed dangerously on the threshold, but stayed on his feet. Gilota felt someone else's painful attack of dizziness and cut it off. The patient could have experienced this himself. Unpleasant, but not life-threatening.

The man looked around the room with a confused and wary look and walked towards the table. The shirt, which was the right width at the shoulders, still hung like a bag on him; his pants were held in place only by a tightened belt. With a sharp movement, he pulled out a chair at the other end of the table, away from the witches, sat down heavily and grabbed his head with both hands. Tangled hair obscured her face, and Gilota was still afraid to pull the invisible thread and open herself to other people's sensations. She expected the man to say at least something, but he lowered his hands and just as silently stared towards the curtained window.

"Okay..." said Gilota, lowering her voice without knowing why, "let's try again." Try to concentrate.

Isa tried honestly. Two of the three apples exploded, and when the third had only a few seconds left to exist, the man suddenly stood up, reached over the table and passed his palm over the doomed fruit. He froze for a moment, so that Gilote had time to seem as if he was listening to the effect of the spell being repeated by Isa, and suddenly abruptly pulled his hand away. The apple exploded.

- Oh, Abyss! Sorry! - Isa exclaimed in fear.

The man sat back, carefully covering the brand with his palm, and did not even look in her direction.

"You didn't feel anything," Gilota told him. — The mark did not respond.

She wanted to say it as a question, but it came out as a statement. Obviously not worth answering, because she saw everything herself. Embarrassed, Isa began to lay out the remaining apples from the bundle. And Gilota suddenly thought about how tired she was of this.

"I don't like stupid visual examples, girl, but apparently I'll have to." Do you know what the mark on this man's face means?

Isa looked away from the apples and shuddered as if, because of such a tactless question, the man could jump up and attack both of them with his fists.

"He was a sorcerer," she answered quietly.

-What do you think happened to him?

She did not understand what they wanted from her, and clear irritation was already beginning to break through the feeling of guilt. Incontinent child, why should she talk about the highest levels of magic?

— Did you like to fuck other people's wives and got caught right by the wife of Prosecutor Tamsen?

In a different situation, Gilota would have been able to appreciate the joke.

- No. I'm not interested in the preconditions, but the consequences. Will you give it another try?

Isa tensed. The first apple in the row burst and scattered across the table. It was followed ten moments later by the second.

- I give up. Was he also bad at handling apples?

Gilota allowed herself to grin, suddenly thinking that in some ways this might actually be the case.

"He was an experienced fighter. But I let people defeat me, girl. This means I missed something important. This means that I was not thinking about what I should have been thinking about at that moment.

The man looked up at her, and Gilota caught a look that was very familiar to her from her previous life. Even if Sir Thomas Wyatt never returns, at least a part of him is firmly rooted in this body. The trouble is different. This is a human body. There is nothing left in it anymore.

Gilota turned away and continued:

- Yes, there are circumstances in which attention to the details of the world around you can save your life. For example, allow you to calculate an ambush. But you may face a fate far worse than death if squeaks, a slight breeze, or thoughts of a hearty meal distract you and you warm the enemy's long johns instead of frying the moody. A moment should be enough to tune in.

Isa shuddered again when the four remaining apples began to boil at the same time.

- Clean up and leave. You'll be back tomorrow.

While the girl was scraping the apple porridge from the table, Gilota went to the window. The tramps sitting at the old pedestal had already disappeared somewhere.

Gilota would not have been able to sincerely answer one simple question for herself - why did she do it? She didn't pass by, leaving the past in the past. Weaved a healing spell on blood instead of bleeding an old enemy. After all, this was exactly what he had been waiting for from her all this time. Yes, that would be dishonest. On the other hand, who in this world has been saved by honesty and righteousness? Being honest is a sign of stupidity incompatible with life, and yet another proof of this theory sits behind her back and tries to pretend that he is not there. The explanation here must be different.

However, the insincere answer will suffice for now.

She heard the girl say goodbye. With a quiet rustle she picked up the basket. The door slammed shut. There was silence in the room.

"You can leave too if you want," said Gilota.

"I don't think my wish can mean anything here," the man answered. "It's in your power to make sure I can't escape."

- Is there somewhere to run? — Gilota was sincerely surprised.

She didn't cast any spells, she didn't put a spell on the door, she didn't put chains on her purchase, she even took off the collar right away, albeit out of urgent need, but she didn't buy a new one to replace it. He himself had already realized that they wouldn't keep him here by force, but he still couldn't keep his mouth shut. It's immediately obvious that he now feels much safer than he did a quarter of an hour ago. And Gilota suddenly realized that this was something of a test. The man is just trying to provoke her. Cause anger, force him to behave as he expects.

Gilota walked across the room and sank into a chair with great pleasure. And the next thing you know, your legs will stop holding you up. Tired, very tired. The man watched her every move expectantly. And instead of answering he said:

— Are you gathering a coven?

But here comes the testing of the boundaries of what is permitted...

- It's none of your business.

- Then maybe you can show me your hand?

Gilota chuckled. She herself saw that a wet spot clearly appeared on the dark sleeve of the dress. It was time to do the dressing.

"You can ask your questions only when you answer mine."

It seemed that the hanging tension could be felt, like the opening of the Abyss or someone else's magical flow.

- What happened to you? - Gilota repeated the most important question.

The man stubbornly pursed his lips and looked away. He sat there for a long time, staring into space. It began to seem to Gilota that nothing would come of this. It's one thing to suffer because of your mistakes. And it's quite another to talk about what a fool he was and how he dug his own grave with his own hands. Then the man exhaled quietly and slouched further.

"I was deceived," he finally spoke. "Then they forced me to give up the witchcraft source. Did you know this is possible? But some of Colette's people are quite good at this.

Part 7

There was a warm kitchen fume with the stuffy smell of herbs in the house. The air in the kitchen became damp and sticky, the stove tiles crackled from the heat. Vessels with water and bath infusions were boiling on the coals, and Gilota, fussing around the stove, regretted with all her heart that she had let Isa go early. On the other hand... The man, having parted with his clothes, did not feel any embarrassment, but it is unlikely that his body could now be considered a suitable spectacle for a young and, in general, not yet very spoiled person. Surely Isa herself would have wanted to run away.

Gilota glanced sideways at the man. He looked relaxed, and this alarmed her more and more. Sitting on a bench, he tried to use a comb to deal with his hair, which had fallen into coarse tangles.

"We have to cut everything," he said, catching her gaze. - Give me the knife.

He pulled at his braids and imitated the movement of the blade with his slightly trembling hand.

- But this...

- Superstition.

A northerner can cut off his hair at the root only if he is preparing to take his own life. Suicide in those parts is an action that is overgrown with many signs and beliefs, and one of them says that there is no greater dishonor than taking one's own life; the spirit of the suicide will forever remain tied to the place of death. Only if he cuts off his hair and burns it will he gain some kind of freedom. But it will never be reborn again. For the first time, Gilota thought that if this was not a simple barbaric tale, but the law of local magic, then she would not be able to predict how it would end. The spirits of the northern coasts are extremely touchy.

- No, it's not worth it. I'll think of something. First, you need more hot water to wash away all the dirt.

- For what?..

Gilota looked at the man in surprise before realizing what he was talking about.

"You still haven't explained what all this is for," he said. - Treat, dress, feed, wash. It's unlikely that you feel sorry for all your enemies; you don't look like a compassionate nun.

She shrugged and took the comb from him. I noticed in passing that the man became wary when she walked behind him.

- Compassion? - Gilota asked mockingly. - Yes, I'm not one of those who is capable of pity, but do you really need someone else's compassion? It always seemed to me that pity is the worst of humiliations for a person of a noble and warlike breed. Albeit involuntary, albeit with good intentions.

Thoughtfully weighing his long dark hair in her palm, she now clearly saw threads of gray hair. Another sign of the times, which she forgot about out of habit. It's easy to lose count of the years when they have no power over you.

Gilota stuck a comb into her hair and entered into an unequal battle with the tangles. The man hissed through his teeth, and small debris fell onto the cleanly swept floor.

"Now I'll do what I can, after water we'll try again," explained Gilota and continued the interrupted explanations: "No, I don't feel sorry for you." What happened was natural. The matter was probably decided according to human law, your mark is proof of this. As for my goals, I need someone to help me with my work and for... some delicate matters. I've been thinking about hiring someone like this for a long time, but it just so happened - I found you and bought you. This is even better, because the mercenary can escape, but you are too honest and probably won't even try. The fact that I care about you now, consider it an investment. It won't be of any benefit to me if the city guard confuses you with a shaggy northern barbarian and hacks you to death on the spot.

Gilota did not expect this, but the man grinned. All that remained was to find out whether this was a sudden manifestation of self-irony or the first sign of an approaching attack of madness.

"I think you have exaggerated hopes for me that are not destined to come true," he expressed a completely reasonable thought.

- Maybe. But this can only be verified in practice.

The man fell silent for a long time, lowering his head. The bones of the back protruded under the pale skin, lined with such scars that Gilota understood at first glance that no amount of effort could heal such permanent scars. Sighing heavily, she leaned over and pressed her chest against his back, feeling through the thick fabric of her dress how the muscles turned to stone from the touch, her body tense. But the man did not try to push her away, did not even move away, but only froze, holding his breath.

"It's okay," she said almost in a whisper, hugging him by the shoulders. - What is bothering you so much now?

Compared to her, he seemed so huge and strong... Not for the first time, Gilota was surprised at how strong men are on the outside, and how this strength plays against them, as soon as someone lets them feel helpless and despair.

"Show me what you did," he asked.

Leaning onto his shoulders, Gilota extended her hand. The man took her wrist and, with ridiculous caution, began to unlace her narrow sleeve. In the light of the fire from the stove, it became clear that the bandage had long been saturated with something dark and sticky. The man unwound it and gasped in surprise.

"This... It must hurt so much..." he muttered in shock and turned his gaze to his own hand, as if he was seeing the wound healing on it for the first time.

Then he felt his throat, apparently not really understanding that this was the least of the fuss.

- It's strange that you haven't realized yet - with me everything is a little different than with other people. It will heal in a couple of days, you just need to get a good night's sleep.

"I understand why your Raven seemed immortal," said the man. "Almost."

- Yes. It took so long to kill him that at some point he probably regretted getting involved with you.

"He knew what he was getting into." But you hardly understood everything, Thomas.

The man shuddered slightly at this address. Gilota walked around the bench and stood in front of him, smiling, meeting his wary gaze.

- In fact, you probably have the wrong opinion about how it works. No wonder, because you slept through the most interesting part. Check this out!

She gently grabbed his chin, forcing him to raise his head.

- What you...

- Shhhh.

For a moment, Gilota simply peered into the long-forgotten, too-changed face, trying to assess whether it would be disgusting to her. And I realized - no. Not at all. Biting her tongue forcefully, she immediately felt her mouth filling with blood.

- What are you doing? - he asked stubbornly.

Leaning down, Gilota kissed him. The lips were tightly compressed, cold and hard. The man tried to pull away, but she put her hand in his hair and squeezed until it hurt. Gasping, he parted his lips. Gilota almost lost her balance from the sudden attack of lightheadedness.

The fire in the stove flared as if it was trying to break free, and then an oncoming gust knocked it onto the coals.

Gilota straightened up. The man opened his cloudy eyes. Blinked. His gaze slowly cleared, with unusual attention he looked around the surrounding space, the low ceiling, shelves, painted tiles on the stove, and froze, catching something in the air that was inaccessible to ordinary eyes.

"That can't be true..." the man whispered. - Do you really feel all this all the time?

"Well, that's it, I did it," Gilota realized with surprise.

It remained to be seen what would happen next.

* * *

The man slept, lost in the days and nights changing somewhere too far from him. During his waking moments, he had no desire to understand what was happening around him.

Once he tried to count the days by feeding, but he lost the first time after seventy, due to some strange fever that deprived him of consciousness for several days, the second time he simply gave up at forty. Only once, as if for the first time looking at his monstrously long nails, feeling his grown hair and beard, did he realize how many days he had spent in captivity. He was simply buried behind bars and forgotten forever. And time, offended by the disdainful attitude towards itself, no longer wanted to take it into account and slipped out of our hands. It flowed somewhere, but for him it froze forever. He no longer counted on any changes in his life, so he remained indifferent to it.

Strange, but now they took care of him all the time. Most of the time he simply lay in the warmth, watching through half-closed eyelids blurry movements, shadows, red lights in the mouth of the stove. Two barely audible female voices conferred above him, trying to ask some questions.

"Drink," he asked in a whisper, and they immediately brought him, first water, then diluted wine.

"What's wrong with him, mother?" - asked one voice.

"In my opinion, insight sometimes fails you, Isa. He's relaxing".

"He's been sleeping for the third day in a row."

"Well, that means he'll look fresh and well-rested later."

At some point, he opened his eyes and sat up, throwing the blanket to the floor. My feet touched the cleanly scrubbed floorboards. Opposite the pushed benches, covered with soft cloth, which served as his bed, a fire was burning in the stove and something was being cooked in a smoked pot. The stove was large, lined with painted tiles. It can be seen that the house once belonged to a rich gentleman, and the kitchen was wide, but now it is filled with mismatched cabinets that have clearly seen better days, and under the ceiling on outstretched lines hung drying clothes, fragrant bunches of herbs and branches, among which a faded dried rowan, and some rag knots. Heaps of dishes were piled on the table.

For some time he looked in surprise at his clean underpants and shirt, and at the healing purple scar stretching along his forearm. And then the door creaked, and a witch appeared on the threshold of the kitchen. Seeing her, he shuddered slightly. I realized that I had relaxed too much and had managed to forget whose house I was in. The witch just nodded to him, slipped past and fussed around the stove.

- How do you feel? Does anything else hurt, is there a feeling of heaviness somewhere or are the muscles cramped?

But no, he felt as if he had already died - nothing hurt.

"But you're just an ordinary city witch," he said.

- Yes. You sound too surprised.

"I think the last time I saw you was...

"Nothing contributes more to a change in lifestyle," the witch interrupted him, "than an untimely death." You know, I was never of royal blood. Now it's clear that there was no point in starting.

He felt a vague chill in his chest. Before him was a woman who had sat on the throne for seventy years. Even now she looks no more than in the first ceremonial portrait, which the palace invaders burned on that memorable day... Lost in thought, he sighed heavily. He lost track of the years and no longer knows how much time has passed, how long the new Emperor has been on the throne. But it does not matter. It is important that now the witch indirectly confirmed in her own words that she had a long life before her reign.

- Who are you?

- Witch.

- This doesn't explain anything. If you want me to follow your orders... I need to know more.

"What a pity that I'm not going to satisfy your curiosity." I'll tell you everything you need to know in due time. Are you going to have dinner?

Listening to himself, he involuntarily sniffed the air through his nose, and the aroma wafting in the kitchen made his insides clench painfully. It would be foolish to deny the obvious.

— Yes.

The dishes clanged. Such a simple home sound.

- Sorry, the girl gets to the kitchen rubble no more than once a week. So...

He was ready for anything. That they will now give him a moldy cracker with the wish of bon appetit, or force him to wash all the dishes in order to work off the upcoming feeding, since he has already been told that he should become an assistant.

- Hold it.

The witch handed him a folded towel and placed a bowl on top filled to the brim with meat brew.

— Until Isa clears away the barricade on the table, he goes out to eat wherever he has to. Be careful, don't spill it.

The warning was unnecessary, because in surprise he squeezed the vessel as if it might break free. The witch, meanwhile, picked up a tray with another bowl and disappeared into the corridor. Footsteps tapped on the creaking floorboards, the door slammed, and it became very quiet.

Loneliness turned out to be very useful, because it suddenly became apparent that he had forgotten how to eat carefully.

* * *

The man jumped up, instantly shaking off the dream, because in this dream he imagined a loud panicked knock, and he was ready to hear the doors breaking and the maids screaming, and strangers armed people breaking into the house to arrest Sir Thomas Wyatt on charges of using prohibited witchcraft and high treason. He rolled head over heels from the unusual narrow bench onto the floor and only then, hitting his side on the floor, did he suddenly realize that they were actually knocking. The door below shakes and clangs. And they scream at the top of their voices:

- Open up, Sage!

Light, quick steps tapped along the corridor, the stairs creaked, and the bolt clanged below. The screams became louder, and frightened voices muttered behind the wall.

The kitchen door swung open, and a witch appeared on the threshold, wearing a long undershirt, covered only with a knitted scarf, with a glass lantern and a backpack in her hands. She rushed along the shelves, raking up some packages and bottles. She rushed back, but suddenly tripped over his legs.

- Why are you rubbing the floor with your butt?! Skip it! - she ordered and immediately yelled somewhere into the corridor: - Marco, take some coal, we'll have to heat the water!

- What's happening?

Although, the answer was obvious - some kind of trouble. A stinking man in rags burst into the kitchen, grabbed buckets behind the stove, and rushed back into the corridor. The witch only waved away the question.

- Faster! Faster! - screamed frightened voices.

- What's happened? I can help!

The witch turned around already on the threshold and looked at him with a strange look.

- Help? - she asked again. - Well, let's go, you can help...

Not understanding what was happening and who all these people were, he still rushed after them, forgetting to throw his cloak over his shoulders. Down the stairs, through the door. The icy air whipped into my face and the pavement burned my bare feet. He could not remember whether he now had shoes, and was glad that he had gone without them for a long time and had time to get used to them. The light of a lantern was rushing ahead; to keep up with it, you had to run, and he rushed without making out the road. Dark gateways and shuttered windows flashed by. Then they all folded, and he folded.

Narrow gateway, basement door. A monstrous stench hit my nose.

- Here!

There was a roar and terrible swearing.

- Let me in, dogs! Let me go, it hurts! Oh my gosh, I'll die right now! Ah-ah-ah!

The woman screamed as if she was being beaten.

The basement turned out to be large and dark, with tiny dirty windows and a cold stove in the corner. In front of the stove, a woman was lying in a heap of tousled and blood-smeared rags. She screamed and desperately fought off the man and woman holding her hands. The witch settled herself between her spread legs and thoughtfully began to press her ugly huge belly.

He froze in horror: he had never seen men allowed to see a woman in labor. The mere thought of it seemed sacrilege. The witch turned around, looking straight at him in the twilight:

- Come on, drown, put on some water to heat! - she ordered and immediately shouted: - Marco, pour coal and bring water!

Not understanding what was happening, the man still rushed to the stove. Marco handed him a hewn flint, but it almost jumped out of his shaking hands, and the rag did not want to be used. He heard the witch curse at him and snap her fingers. The man screamed in surprise and pain as the flames escaped from his fingers and attacked the coals.

- Pick her up!

"Don't get bloated!" No-e-et!

- Lift up, put the sheet on!

More squealing and screaming.

Marco brought the buckets down on the stove, nearly dousing the fire.

- It's up against it! - declared the witch, trying to shout down the hysterical woman in labor. - We need to get it!

"Nena-ah!.." the woman squealed, but one of the men covered her mouth with the sleeve of his jacket. She grabbed the dirty fabric with her teeth, began to flail like a dog and desperately kick her legs.

- Bring the tub! Hey, are you deaf?! Thomas!

The man perked up and began rummaging through the rubbish piled up around the stove in search of a vessel. Then Marco appeared again, pulled the tub out from under the bench and rushed to the woman in labor.

- Thomas! Thomas! - the witch shouted impatiently.

He rushed to the call, slipped barefoot and almost fell - something red and sticky was trampled on the floor.

- Hold your leg!

The woman in labor kicked him in the head, then in the shoulder. The strength in her turned out to be immeasurable. The man finally caught her by the ankle, leaned on her, breathing heavily, and saw with horror how, right in front of his eyes, the witch thrust her hand at the woman in labor... She immediately fell on top, blocking her view and plunging her elbow into her stomach, but even a moment of this spectacle was enough . He turned away, feeling a sticky, sick lump rise in his throat. The light of the lanterns before my eyes swayed and turned around...

And then the world shook with a powerful blow. The slap made my ear ring.

— Thomas!

The man was surprised to realize that this was his name, and now he was being called, but as if from afar. He was sitting on a dirty floor in some basement. Nearby, a baby was crying shrilly. The second, quiet and somewhat shriveled, the witch held up with her legs and shook rhythmically as if she was going to hit the stone floor, but still couldn't decide. Finally, she shook him especially hard and slapped him on the back. The child made a terrible dull sound, spat sticky mucus onto the floor and immediately screamed.

There were groans and curses all around.

"You have twins," the witch said to the woman huddled on the floor.

She howled, smearing tears across her flushed, grimy face.

- Well, that's enough. Let's get to your bleeding now.

"Don't...nadova..." the woman moaned.

Just to avoid looking at it, the man began to look around furtively and only now realized that they were visiting in a clearly bad place. The dim light snatched from the darkness roughly hewn rugs, littered with rags and intertwined bodies wrapped in rags. Someone was sleeping, someone was looking with interest at the action unfolding by the stove. The fire heated the air in the basement, and it seemed that the stench of unwashed bodies became even thicker.

"I don't want-u-u-u..." howled the woman on the floor.

The man, whom the witch called Marco, tried to console her.

— Ku-u-u-uda...

The witch, wrapping the child in a clean rag she had brought with her, bent down and put her hand on her shoulder.

"If you strangle me again, I'll die," she said in a voice that didn't waver.

Then there was more fuss. The babies were washed, the mother in labor was given an unbearably smelly brew...

It was even colder outside, or maybe it only seemed so, because now they were not running, but were walking at a calm pace. The man was carrying buckets and a sack, the witch walked ahead, staggering from fatigue.

The horror he experienced, never seen before, seemed to tear him out of his stupor and sharpened all his senses. The trembling in my hands slowly went away. He felt the prickly drizzle falling from the sky settle on his face, how the icy air made its way under his shirt, and slowly, as if he was regaining consciousness, emerging from oblivion, he realized that he was alive. He is even almost free, although he is essentially in slavery. But never in recent years had he felt so free. And so happy - just from the thought that he had left the creepy basement and would soon return to where it was warm and calm.

-What was this place? - he decided to ask.

The foul smell was absorbed into his clothes and skin, and it seemed that now he would never wash off.

"Marco's sleeping cellar," the witch answered with a heavy sigh. - The cheapest in the area. This company is more united than any knightly order.

He paused, not knowing how to ask the next question, then finally decided:

"Has this woman killed her children before?"

"Yes, she strangled the first one, Marco didn't have time to follow her."

- But why?

"She said that she couldn't feed him, but that's a lie to make him feel sorry for him." In fact, Marco was going to sell it, she was scared and didn't want to give it away. Then she asked for such a share that the deal would not have worked out. And this time - twins. Marco was lucky.

The man thought he had misheard.

- Sell? - he asked stupidly.

"Yes," the witch confirmed with irritation in her voice. - Sell. Am I speaking too quietly?

- No. But I do not understand.

- What is unclear? Marco and his men are chimney sweepers who work for Eddrick and enter houses through rooftops. You can teach a child to do this, but it takes many years. It is more profitable for Marco to sell the babies to places where they can be used right now - to beggars. With a child in their arms, they are served more. Twins are like a gift from Heaven for him. They even came running after me so as not to lose the goods. Marco is now obliged to give me a share of the sale.

- Oh, Abyss... It's... You...

He fell silent, realizing that he could not find the words. I tried to find somewhere inside anger, hatred... at least something, but there was only emptiness and a single frightened thought beating in my head:

"Where am I?.. Where did I end up?.."

For a moment I woke up from a terrible dream only to fall deeper into a nightmare with no bottom in sight.

"Welcome to the world of people, Thomas," said the witch. "He will welcome you with open arms."

Part 8

When the sun had just passed midday, there was another knock on the door, and Gilota, cursing the whole wide world, realized that she would not have to rest today. The visitors, a couple of well-dressed hillbillies, had come from afar and were now determined to get the most out of their trip to the city. The hillbillies had the usual problems. The cattle often began to get sick, whether one of the neighbors had caused damage, the soil in the fields was tired and each harvest was harder than the previous one. Gilota listened, nodded, and looked among the bottles and bags on the shelf for the necessary ingredients for the next brew. Soon a sour stench hung in the room - when the smells from different boiling vessels were mixed, something definitely bad came out, but they didn't care, as long as the hillbillies didn't confuse later what to pour into the pig trough and what to leave to the earthen demon in a bottle and with a snack.

"But this is my niece, Tessie, who will walk down the aisle in the spring," explained the portly village woman, untying the knot she had pulled from her bosom. - You should take a look too, even if only a year in advance.

The package contained carved wooden beads. Gilota extended her hand, the village woman placed the jewelry into her palm, awkwardly touching the skin with her fingers petrified from calluses...

In the darkness that clouded the eyes, a flame flared up.

The sky turned black with soot, and the world below it was on fire. Houses and barns were burning, the earth itself was burning, and the flames rolled along the grass, devouring bodies lying among the dead wood. And the spilled blood turned black from the heat, baked, and formed timid flames amid the general conflagration. It seemed to Gilota that the beads lying in her palm also turned into hot coals, and only good endurance allowed her not to throw them away in horror, and even maintain a calm, inscrutable face. The thread of this woman's life was only one, and it stretched into that fiery world, where it broke off among the fire and acrid black smoke.

"You can't see through the thing," Gilota lied. - Give me your hands, I'll look through you.

The woman immediately extended her palm, the man hesitated a little. It is clear that he treated the city witch with slight distrust. Gilota prepared herself internally, but still the vision stunned her with its brightness, scorched her with a heat that did not yet exist. These people haven't had a year, only eight months left. She tried to snatch at least some signs from what she saw in order to understand what would happen, but there were too few of them. Just a brief moment of some kind of war, rolling like a fiery wheel through a tiny village, lost in the endless expanse of the current borders of the empire.

"Everything will be fine for her, and for you too." Just don't delay the wedding, as soon as it gets warmer, celebrate it.

- What about the guy? — the village woman became worried.

- Good, hard-working. You won't find anything better.

She sprinkled questions, Gilota gave meaningless answers, but at that time she was thinking about her own things. In the end, even if a person thinks that he has come to a witch who sees the future in order to be warned and fully prepared to face troubles and adversity, in reality this is not the case. The abyss will never show what is truly important to see. Seers are turned to for hope for the best. And this is the main thing that should be generously given to the client in response to any questions. Yes, the earth demon will no longer spoil and destroy crops if he is properly fed. Yes, your wealth in your house will increase next season, and Tessie's niece will be happy.

Another thought flashed through my mind that it would be nice if the villagers were satisfied with the trip and recommended the witch to some neighbors. Maybe through them it will be possible to look into the fire again and learn more about the coming disaster. After all, in those lands there was no war even when it seemed to be everywhere.

When a couple of villagers left her house, the sky had already dimmed and dusk was slowly gathering on the streets. Gilota listened from the door and went to the kitchen, guided by the sounds of a strange fuss. There, perched with her feet on the edge of the table and carefully stepping over the dishes, Isa collected cobwebs from the top shelves of the cabinets. The selected hem of the dress fluttered dangerously close to the flasks and bottles, threatening to knock something over on the floor with an awkward movement. But the biggest problem was that Isa was alone in the kitchen.

Gilota walked through the rooms to make sure that no, there was no one else on her floor. She returned to the kitchen.

- Where is Thomas?

At the sound of her voice, Isa twitched and almost fell to the floor.

- W-who? — she asked again in fear and immediately realized: "The man left."

- Where? - Gilota was surprised.

- Outside. "I took my cloak and went out," Isa answered, already guessing that something bad had happened. "I thought he was on your instructions, mother." I was also surprised, but he looked like he knew what he was doing...

There was no time to listen to excuses.

- For a long time?

Isa shrugged her shoulders guiltily.

"An hour ago," she suggested. - Seems.

* * *

Many different inventions flashed through Gilota's head as she rushed around the neighborhood. "Round, hopeless, stuffed fool!" immediately gave way to an angry one: "Well, wait a minute, I'll find it, I'll put a leash on you so that you can't step over the threshold, you'll immediately collapse in writhing!", and then it will go back to "What was I thinking, you foolish dog?"

She began her search from nearby gateways. In the alley that ended in a dead end, there was no one except a tattered gray cat. In the next one, leading to dilapidated utility sheds, some tramps were drinking one bottle for four. Gilota called out to them, and their equally grimy, angry faces stared at her. However, having recognized the local sorceress, they immediately relaxed and tried to merge with the area. Even if such people robbed someone to buy their booze, it was unlikely to be a former knight who didn't have a penny in his pockets. Spitting in frustration, Gilota closed her eyes and concentrated. The invisible thread, already thinned to the limit, tightened, but the sensations turned out to be surprisingly peaceful. Frustration, despondency, oppressive fatigue and, just a little - anger.

Following the thread that was melting before her eyes, Gilota went out to the square, crossed the space paved with chipped stones, avoiding dubious companies and beggars sitting anywhere, dived into the passage between multi-story buildings, got out onto a narrow street, where dirt mixed with slop munched underfoot, and high Overhead, out of reach of thieves, washed sheets were drying. The porches of the back entrances, decorated with forged and carved railings, indicated that the multi-story buildings were inhabited by "decent" people, even despite the close proximity to slums. This is how the New City is - everything is mixed up here.

Behind the houses there was a wide avenue. And at the end of the passage, leaning his shoulder against the wall, stood a man and from the deep shadows looked at the hurrying passers-by, the passing carriages, carts, and horsemen.

- You're crazy! - Gilota exclaimed in horror. - Put on your hood immediately!

Looking back, the man looked her up and down.

"Is it too obvious that I'm a shaggy northern barbarian?"

- No. But at first glance it is clear that you were tried for malicious witchcraft.

The man winced painfully.

"That's it," was all he said.

Standing on tiptoe, Gilota pulled his hood, covering his face.

- Let's go to.

- Where?

- Look around. Isn't that what you're here for?

And for some reason, both simultaneously looked towards the avenue glowing with lights. Lanterns shone, lights flickered in shop windows, and dozens of windows poured warm yellow light onto the twilight street. A motley crowd floated past the dark passage; no one paid attention to the couple hiding in the darkness.

"It seemed to me that everything was supposed to change like that," the man said unexpectedly.

"From what? The tails on the coats have become shorter, and this season milliners are recommending emerald shades and stand-up collars," Gilota thought mockingly, but remained silent. Everything she could say seemed too inappropriate. The last fibers of the magical thread were melting, and she still felt too well someone else's hopeless melancholy. You probably have to feel very lonely to share your experiences with your former enemy.

"It turns out I just forgot a lot."

Gilota looked attentively at the man, but he never noticed, looking at the street lights in fascination.

"Over time, memories become blurred and lose clear details," he continued. "If I even wanted to imagine a street, it would only be an ugly fake." The world was distorted even in my sleep. And now reality seems too... There is too much here.

"Let's go," Gilota suggested again. "I think I know a place we should visit first." There are times when reality needs some distortion.

* * *

Bursts of violin music and ringing laughter, the roar of many voices overtook a couple of passers-by wandering along a narrow street long before a porch with slippery, suspiciously sticky steps came into view. Above the entrance there was a painted sign, barely visible in the darkness: "Rose hip and sword." The name hinted at the family coat of arms and military glory of the current great Emperor, and the tavern under the sign was, in fact, not the worst establishment in the area. Considering that nearby there were all hot spots, where the city guards rarely visited, trying in every possible way to avoid unnecessary troubles. At least in Briar and the Sword the drink did not taste like urine, and when food was served to the table, it was not cat or dog meat, and the cow, which previously carried this meat on its bones, died at the hands of the butcher, and did not die from some illness. And the fact that Gilota is able to conjure mad cow disease into the owner of the tavern had a surprisingly beneficial effect on the quality of service.

The floor was covered with straw. There were long tables under the low ceiling, each with several oil lamps burning. The tavern turned out to be crowded with people. Lively girls in ugly open dresses scurried between the tables, already habitually dodging pinches and steps. Men's voices and women's laughter seemed deafening; groups of drunken visitors chattered, not listening, but only trying to shout over each other.

- This is where you can definitely take off your hood! - Gilota tried to explain, although she was not sure that the man heard her in the surrounding noise.

She moved between the tables, trying to look at a vacant corner somewhere, when one of the visitors suddenly turned around and grabbed her hand.

- Noble lady, let me invite you!

Turning her gaze, Gilota saw the face of the big Hugo grinning with a friendly smile. The venerable thief elbowed his neighbor forcefully, and a feverish movement immediately swept across the bench near the table. Gilota nodded gratefully and hurried to settle into the vacant seat, pulling the man along with her. He sat down on the very edge and looked around at the company at the table with a wary gaze, in which hostility was too clearly visible.

A girl immediately appeared nearby, lowered two mugs onto the tabletop, and briefly bowed her head.

- From the owner to you, madam witch! - she said loudly.

"Tell the owner my gratitude," answered Gilota, taking several copper coins from her wallet and laying them on the table. "We'll also have dinner, whatever the owner recommends, and then we'll see."

The girl once again made a bow, swept away the coins with a subtly quick movement and immediately seemed to disappear into thin air.

A heated discussion of some pressing matters was in full swing at the table. The big Hugo, raking the air with his huge paws, boasted of how cleverly he had beaten some presumptuous competitor. Sitting opposite Eddrick, skinny, red-haired, with a wide, gap-toothed smile, nodded approvingly and assented:

- These pigs, look what they came up with! Share it, you see! Next time they poke their noses in, they'll share their innards with me!

"Easy there," Hugo besieged him. "If our witch lady hadn't cast a good amulet for you, you'd already be lying in a ditch with your intestines spilled out." Or he received a hemp collar as a gift from Tamsen the dog.

The girl reappeared and lowered two clay bowls onto the table. Gilota began to eat, but then glanced sideways at her companion - the man sat motionless, listening to the conversation at the table, and did not pay attention to the bowl of hot meat.

- What are you doing? - she hissed in his ear.

The man did not touch the food brought, but he drained the mug in one fell swoop. Gilota looked at this, called the girl and asked her to bring her companion something stronger. The next mug followed the first one at the same speed, as if it contained water and not mash. Gilota asked the girl for a third mug, but before moving it to the man, she made a subtle movement of her fingers over the drink. This already seemed funny enough. Not that she really wanted her companion to end up drunk... but some things are perceived better when the mind is pliable.

He reached for another portion, but hesitated and suddenly looked at her:

- Is this the same money?

The man's voice suddenly became tense. Gilota turned to him and was surprised to realize from his tense posture that he was preparing to get up and leave at any moment.

- What are you talking about? — she clarified carefully.

— About your share from the sale of babies. And this one, on the contrary, is the same Eddrick? I'd rather stay hungry.

Gilota smiled tightly.

- No, I won't have that money earlier than in a couple of weeks. So you can eat in peace. Or... And if I tell you how I earned those coins with which I saved you, and it's some terrible thing, I suppose you'll return to your previous owner? It seemed to me that some moral dilemmas had already resolved themselves. You look much better and more confident than when we first met. So why these ostentatious gestures? Let's quickly get drunk and get away from here.

She tried to press herself against his shoulder, but the man only shook his head gloomily. Gilota moved closer, accidentally touching his hand - he moved away.

"This is all wrong, from beginning to end."

And again he drained the mug in one fell swoop. Gilota noticed some kind of evil light in his eyes. However, she is not alone.

- What do you want?! - Eddrick barked from the other side of the table, who clearly didn't like the intense and angry look on his person.

The man smiled.

"Oh, the Abyss," thought Gilota.

- Well, why are you staring?! — Eddrick did not let up.

"Relax," the extremely perspicacious Hugo tried to calm him down. "This is the lady witch's man, don't interfere with him."

It could still have ended harmlessly, although the retinue of thieves seated at the table had already become silent, trying to understand what was happening, and all eyes were fixed on the "Madam Witch" and his companion. They also looked with interest from the neighboring tables.

"I want to and I'm staring," the man said, smiling wider. "I've never seen a talking pile of crap before."

Eddrick roared, swung, and threw his mug at him, which flew over the table, splashing the remains of the drink. The former knight put out his hand, making a strange gesture, and Gilota realized in horror that he was trying to hang a magical shield. But the man came to his senses, with a deft movement he caught the vessel flying at him and threw it back so sharply that Eddrick had no chance to dodge. The mug crashed into his head, the thief tumbled off the bench and fell to the floor.

Gilota appreciated the throw and immediately began to look around, looking for a way to escape. The tavern became suspiciously quiet. Among the crowd of visitors, lovers of a good fight were already looking at each other.

"Chill, sorcerer," said Hugo. - Let's calm down.

"I forgot to ask you, you filthy rabble."

Gilota grabbed the man's hand, but he impatiently pushed her away and stood up, looking at the crowd frozen at the table. It even seemed to her that now he would make some kind of insulting speech for the entire local society, saying that the place for such things was on the gallows and in the garbage dumps. But the man simply took the bowl with the untouched food, put it on Hugo's head with a flourish and mockingly patted the big man on the cheek.

"Let's calm down," he suggested carefully.

The world around roared and began to move. An angry howl, the roar of breaking furniture, a multi-voiced female scream...

Gilota had some experience of being present in crowded fights, and therefore understood that it would be safer for a woman of her size to move away and not interfere in such a mess. She dodged some thief thrown to the side and almost stepped on a hysterically screaming girl huddled in the aisle between the shops. Somewhere behind him, the former knight met another enemy with a powerful blow, and he had to dodge the falling body again. Picking up her uncomfortable heavy skirt, Gilota jumped onto the table like a mountain goat and jumped up, clinging to the low hanging ceiling beam. I managed to pull myself up at the last moment - the table below gave way and flew somewhere to the side under the pressure of the human scrum. Gilota grabbed the beam and sat down, looking at the battlefield below with wary curiosity. A couple of frightened peddlers were already hanging nearby.

"No more than half a minute," Gilota thought at the first moment, folding her hands and feeling a still timid fire flaring up in her palm.

But the former knight fought no worse than on the battlefield, and they could not knock him down and beat him even after a minute.

The man threw off his cloak and acquired a weapon when some idiot tried to hit him on the head with a broken table leg, and now he moved like crazy, carrying out attacking maneuvers and writing out volts, dodging the bullies. From the height of her precarious position, Gilota assessed with admiration the possibilities of her acquisition - as if seven years removed from life had never happened. The movements turned out to be so rapid that three losers who decided to stun him from behind were left lying on the floor.

Hugo, who had barely come to his senses and rushed into the attack again, flew to the side with a curled nose and a couple of knocked out teeth. Splashes of blood flew in all directions. The man, without stopping his movement, managed to contrive and forcefully kicked the big man in the head. Over the noise of the fight, one could not hear the snap of a twisted neck. And by the way the nature of the attacks changed, Gilota suddenly realized that poor Hugo would not be the only dead person today. The fleeting murder only provoked the former knight, who clearly intended to die on such an unheroic battlefield.

Luck could not remain on the man's side for long. He stumbled on his own, even without outside help. And then he was hit in the back with a board torn out from somewhere, and then kicked in the stomach... He grabbed his leg and pulled so that the attacker ended up on the floor. He rolled over, crushing him under himself, and began to hit, not paying attention to the blows to his back. The fists were torn to the flesh, the sleeves of the shirt were soaked in blood. In these moments, he resembled not a person, but a demon of destruction filled with hatred, possessing a fragile human shell and ready to tear it apart from the inside with his black power. They dragged him by his hair and clothes, showering him with blows from all sides, but he still growled and tried to get someone.

Gilota closed her eyes, took a deep breath, and spread her palms. A not burning, but dazzlingly bright fire rushed down, hit the seething crowd with a roar and scattered over the fragments of furniture. Absolutely all the people who were in "Rosehip and Sword" instantly had no time for a fight.

Part 9

"You shouldn't have done that," said Gilota, although she understood that now these words made no sense.

From the alley where they had taken refuge, it was clear how the commotion at the porch of the Rosehip and the Sword gradually subsided. Several revelers were left lying in the mud on the pavement, too drunk or beaten to move on their own, or perhaps simply trampled in the general confusion as people fled the witch fire. Only now a detachment of city guards arrived on the street, as if all these armed warriors were standing around the corner and waiting for the moment when the mess would end without them. Not at all confused, they immediately took on everyone who did not have time to run far. Gilota whispered a spell and saw a thin veil, invisible to the average eye, unfold over the shelter in the passage between the houses, making the hidden witch and the former knight inaudible and invisible.

— Did I needlessly offend your dear friends? - the man asked and laughed.

Leaning against the wall, he tried to wipe his dirty face with an equally dirty shirt sleeve. Blood flowed from a broken nose. The laughter was cut short by a hoarse cough. He winced, pressing his hands to his stomach, and spat into the dirt.

- You could have been killed. You had no right... no, you didn't even have a worthy reason to risk your life!

- Enough!

The shout sounded so rude that Gilota was taken aback for several moments, trying to understand whether she had heard commanding notes in the voice of a man who had recently been scared to death by her mere presence nearby.

- What you said?

The man slowly shifted his body weight to his feet and stood up straight, staggering slightly. And he rushed straight at her. From the blow, Gilota slammed her back into the rough wall so that her vision went dark for a moment. The mutilated left hand clumsily but firmly grabbed her throat. The eyes burned with desperate rage. Kicking and clawing, Gilota clung to his arm and tried to loosen her grip, but nothing happened. He loomed over her like a black stone mass, but for some reason he did not try to strangle her or break her larynx. He just looked, grinning. And it became clear that the excitement that had come over him in the tavern did not subside, but only subsided to fall in a second wave.

"I told you to shut your mouth, witch," he muttered through clenched teeth.

Gilota would still not be able to answer - every breath of air was difficult for her. She sincerely regretted that the invisible thread had time to disappear. She herself could barely figure out what was happening. There was now a completely different person in front of her. Bringing a threat. Not rage, not bloodlust, but the dangerous determination of a trapped beast.

"Let me go," she wheezed with difficulty, clinging to his hand and trying to squeeze off the fingers that were causing her pain.

Perhaps he got too carried away, although he probably knew what could happen next. Should have known.

Gilota stopped fighting for air, relaxed and moved her hand to the side with a sharp movement. The man stumbled back screaming. Under the shirt, a bright burn streak flared up and went out. Finally taking a deep breath of air, Gilota caught the thread that had appeared from the infused force and pulled. The man wheezed and fell to his knees.

The man managed to take her by surprise, even frighten her. This turned out to be extremely unpleasant. With vengeful pleasure, Gilota wove a new pass. A flash flashed, another scream echoed in the narrow passage between the walls of the houses, never breaking through the magical veil into the real world.

— Have you regained consciousness, or should I try to wake you up again?

"Well, try it," the man responded hoarsely.

Gilota tilted her head slightly to the side, looking with interest at the man fidgeting on the ground. He sat down with difficulty, leaning his back against the stonework, looking up at the witch.

"You look like you enjoy being hurt."

The man laughed hoarsely.

"Okay, I think this is where we should end our first "outing," said Gilota, trying hard to understand what was happening. - It's time for us to return.

- No.

She might even think that she heard it. But the man did not move. He had no intention of getting up.

- What are you planning?

- Nothing, unlike you. This is the person you need. I don't need a hostess. I changed my mind. I don't want to live among this crap.

Gilota smiled tightly. No matter what else, but in terms of impudence the man sitting in front of her was already quite comparable to the once-living Thomas Wyatt. That's pretty much how he talked in the old days.

"What a pity," he said mockingly, "after all, everything was so well thought out!" Pick up a beaten dog, warm it up, feed it from your hands, caress it so that it can taste human life, become eternally grateful to you and look into your eyes with love. Tell him anything and he'll run to do it, right? But you were wrong! Do you think I'll lose my head from worry and forget who you are? Will I obey only because you paid money for my skin?

Gilota could only grin at such amazing insight.

"Aren't you afraid that I might force you?"

- You can try.

Gilota folded her fingers for another pass. The man held his breath, not taking his eyes off her hand. No, she didn't even hope that he would immediately back down, but he could at least be scared. Instead there was only silent determination. Probably the same feeling with which its acquisition, at the first convenient moment, drove the lancet into my throat.

With a wave of her palm, Gilota shook off the overflowing power. There had been no worthy use for it for a long time; a lot of it had accumulated, and the excess was bursting to the surface.

- Why are you doing it? - she asked. - You act as if we are still enemies, although this is clearly not the case. The world I fought for, the world you fought for, they are both gone. Now there can be no conflict of interests between us. And you complicate everything to the point of open confrontation. What is this for?

The man was silent for a while. Then he said very quietly:

- I dreamed of killing you. I killed you.

- What, would you like to do it again?

- Hardly. Now I don't care anymore. In the world, where are people like this... - he clearly wanted to say something important, but immediately cut himself off. - Doesn't matter. There is nothing left of me. I have nothing to hold on to in this world, nothing to live for. I'm not going to serve you. You can try to force it. You can set it on fire right away. You wasted eight dinars, sorry.

Gilota chose to skip this obvious prick.

"How lovely. You now resemble a small child who sat on the floor and is capricious because he is again forced to eat tasteless porridge."

But she didn't say that out loud either.

"If you think you can't be worse off, there may always be someone unluckier," she said. — There were people who followed you to the end. Your despondency is a betrayal for them. How would that boy squire look at you if he saw his master in this form?

The man shook his head.

"I think the grave worms ate his eyes seven years ago." There was a time when being on my side turned out to be life-threatening. He was not the only one who suffered; they showed me the papers.

- However, he still has a chance to look at you.

He probably didn't immediately understand where she was leading. And he suddenly shuddered and looked at her, although in the thickening darkness of the night it was no longer possible to see her face.

- Was Falco alive?

"I have no idea what his name is, but I think we are talking about the same person."

There was silence. The man tried to get up, grabbing the wall, groaned, and slid into the mud again. Gilota took two steps forward and extended her hand to him. He looked at the palm as if he did not understand the meaning of this gesture. Gilota retreated. The silence had already begun to seem oppressive to her when the man finally asked:

- Why did you choose me?

It took some time to think about the answer.

- We already knew each other. You knew me, I thought it would be easier this way.

"I knew," the man nodded. "I will never forget who you are." But..." he paused, collecting his thoughts, then spoke loudly and confidently: "But if you need something from me, I can do it." Whatever it is. On one condition - in return you help me.

Out of surprise, Gilota could not restrain herself - she chuckled loudly, the corners of her mouth turned up, but at least she managed to contain her laughter.

"It will be beneficial for both of us," the man added.

Just recently he was angry as a devil, but now he didn't seem to care at all that they were laughing at him. However, at that time he hardly had any desire to seek compromises. This means that the matter has finally moved forward.

"It seems I was mistaken in thinking you were reasonable." You really are crazy. What might you need that would be useful to me?

- Who is this Tamsen now, about whom your girl and that bastard in the tavern were talking?

Gilot suddenly became serious.

- Now? This is Chief Prosecutor Recknitz. A great friend of our Emperor Rogir, who appointed him from the capital to our wilderness to restore order. It deals mainly with nobles disloyal to the authorities, but it also gets to the mob. It was he who started the days of mass hangings here.

"The Abyss knows no coincidences," the man muttered. "You wanted to know where my power went?" If I can get to this person, perhaps I can get the answer you need from him.

The idea turned out to be so crazy that even Gilota found it difficult to take it seriously. For some time she simply looked in confusion at the man smeared with mud in the darkness of the gateway, feeling that this strange conversation was tearing her away from reality. The feeling was like in a dream, when the logical world, in the reality of which you managed to believe, suddenly collapses, becoming more and more strange and absurd.

"You're just a person now," she said finally. "You will die if you contact Tamsen."

- I'm human, but you are not. And you can help me," the man answered. — Centuries-old crowns of trees intertwined overhead, grass flooded with water underfoot... black vines in the water...

Gilota froze with surprise, leaned back slightly, and he noticed her confusion.

- You know what I'm talking about, don't you? Got yourself a well-fed... pet? You can take me there, then I won't be helpless.

"He's still very dangerous. And she has enough impudence," thought Gilota, but was not surprised. She accepted this thought easily, even with hidden joy. A man whose life was taken away, turning it into a legend, bailed out to dozens of deceitful bards, and leaving him only a shadow of his former self, in a slave collar, still posed a serious threat to his enemies. She suddenly felt a slight bitterness. How things could have turned out if their relationship had not started with hostility! If only there had been at least one opportunity to join forces in those days!

It turned out to be too interesting.

- How do you know about the creature?

"The Abyss showed it to me in a dream, the night before meeting you." She does not send such visions in vain. Will you take me there?

- Maybe. But you must know that it will require retribution. Now, later, someday in the future. And if you fail, your fate will be sadder than death. You have to think very, very carefully before you make decisions and make such sacrifices. Is it worth it, Thomas?

For the first time she said his name and did not feel internal rejection. On the contrary, right now it seemed right. She was addressing a man she had known for a long time.

A long silence followed. Then the man chuckled dryly.

— Previously, you were more careful in collecting information. And now... in vain I didn't try to find out more about the boy. His name is Falko from Tranfe or Falko Tamsen.

Gilota recalled the age of prosecutor Vimark Tamsen, landowner of Tranfe, and clarified:

- One of the younger ones?

- Yes, the youngest of twelve. But he still tried to gain his father's favor. He didn't understand that he was being lied to. And then I didn't want to believe it, until the last I hoped that it was some kind of terrible mistake. And this was just a correct calculation. Tamsen Sr. determined from the very beginning that he could put on the altar of high goals," Thomas unexpectedly smiled bitterly and added: "You see what sacrifices these people are ready for." And I won't even lose anything I could value. Everything has already been taken away from me.

Gilota stood in the darkness and thought. After all these years, the man's words can be considered true. The ancient creation of the Abyss cannot compare with the sophistication of the human mind.

"I will fulfill your request," she said.

* * *

Even in the square, Gilota felt a strange tension in the air. No obvious signs indicated the presence of danger, and yet there was danger. And it clearly did not come from the tramps hanging around in the area. On the contrary, they were the ones who gave it away. They behaved strangely. The companies that came along the way looked askance at the witch and her companion.

"Something's wrong," Gilota said in a whisper, Thomas heard her and tensed.

She thought briefly that this was an extremely unfortunate moment - he had been beaten up too much in the tavern, he could barely stand on his feet, although he was trying not to show it. If another life-or-death fight happens, then now Thomas will definitely be finished off.

- Don't stay close. Stay back five steps and don't interfere," she ordered.

- Do you feel something? - Thomas asked worriedly.

- No. But this is bad.

From the dimly lit square they turned onto a side street, towards the back door. And it seemed to Gilote that the people who came out to meet her were not hiding near the walls, but were condensed from the darkness reigning in the nooks and crannies of the night. Two, both with weapons. There was no need to even turn around to make sure that the retreat route was cut off.

— Sorceress Almasina Eda?

"Yes," answered Gilota.

She expected some explanation to follow, because the men blocking her path were wearing city guard uniforms. If all this is because of the prank in "Rosehip and the Sword," then the matter can still be resolved peacefully... One of the guards sharply jerked his hand. Gilota felt a push in her chest. And then the thing that hit her flared up like a piece of red-hot iron, gnawing into her flesh. It became impossible to breathe. Grasping the air like a fish thrown out of water, Gilota staggered and could hardly stand on her suddenly weakened legs.

- By the sanction of Mr. Prosecutor Tamsen, you are arrested for malicious witchcraft and the murder of the venerable Erevard Eagle Prim.

A strange fuss, blows, wheezing was heard from behind...

Gilota tried to pull out the artifact stuck into her body and screamed in pain - the fire, bright blue, hostile to her nature, spread to her palm. She pulled harder, feeling the skin give way... The guards grabbed her hands. Howling in pain, Gilota tried to wriggle free.

The head of the guard holding her right hand exploded. Blood and sticky sharp pieces splattered. The second guard quickly rushed forward, drawing a short sword from its sheath and swinging. A scream was heard.

Gilota grabbed the artifact with both hands and pulled with all her might. The pain was as if she had torn a piece of meat out of her body. But the monstrous object remained in his hands. Throwing him aside, Gilota took a deep breath and clenched her fists, feeling the force inside her curling like a tight spring, ready to explode. She raised her hands and let her out.

Time stood still.

In the darkness, the contours of objects fused into the magical field glowed clearly. Isa's body, with its chest cut by a sword, froze in its fall on the dirty pavement, and a guard stood motionless above him, only managing to glance over his shoulder at the detainee who had managed to get rid of the artifact. It is unlikely that he had time to understand what the mistake was. After all, this item could drink an ordinary witch to the bottom and make her completely helpless. The one who handed over the artifact for arrest simply did not imagine the real capabilities of the sorceress Almasina.

Gilota turned around. Thomas was lying on the ground, huddled and covering his injured ribs with his hands. One of the guards standing over him moved his leg back for another blow, the other stepped on the former knight's shoulder.

The burnt palms hurt unbearably. There was a bloody stain on the chest, almost invisible on the black fabric of the torn dress. Gilota felt that the monstrous tension of frozen reality was about to tear her apart from the inside. She raised her hand, pointing her finger at each living guard in turn, and fiery spots flared up on the men's chests. Once upon a time, with the one and only vile feudal lord Akerlea, the former owner of the Recknitz land, it turned out easy, compared to how it had to be done now.

No more than a moment passed in the outside world. Gilota exhaled. Time rushed forward.

Three live fires broke out simultaneously.

Swaying, Gilota blinked rapidly, trying to clear the fog from her head. But she couldn't stay on her feet and fell. Having lost consciousness while still in flight, she did not even feel the impact on the pavement stones.

Part 10

Just before dawn, merchant Goslin looked up from his book, hearing a terrible rumble below. Someone persistently knocked on the door of his shop, most likely even with their foot. Unheard of impudence, which should hardly have been encouraged. Therefore, Goslin just leaned back in his chair, irritably rubbing his aching temples and thinking about how he would refuse to do any business with such an impudent man. The knocking stopped after a couple of minutes. But then it thundered again, with such force that Goslin almost dropped the book in surprise. And he even thought for the first time that a long time ago he should have hired some big security guard in case of such crazy clients. Previously, he relied on the idea that no one in the city would want to have him as an enemy. But it was better to play it safe. Next time.

And now he finally got up from his chair, seriously fearing that in the morning he would have to start fixing the door. He tripped and almost fell head over heels down the stairs, lit the lamp and leaned towards the window. Something black and bulky loomed behind the dirty glass.

- Go away! - Goslin yelled at him.

The dark figure swung forward, and the door shook again from the impact. Dust swirled in the air.

- Get out of here, hanged man! - Goslin demanded and threatened:
- I'm armed!

- But not me! Open, I need help," a hoarse voice came from outside the window. - I am from the witch Almasina.

Hearing this name, Goslin shuddered, frantically wondering how to avoid meeting the strange messenger outside the door and not get any bad consequences because of this.

He immediately realized that the matter was serious, even when the city guard showed up at the shop the day before and began asking questions about trading matters. Extremely bad questions regarding some extremely important clients. Goslin found himself between two fires. He did not want to lie to the envoys of the authorities. But at the same time, he was well aware of what some of his clients could do to himself if it became known that he had disclosed their affairs to third parties. Goslin knew how to keep really important secrets. And he didn't even have to distort the facts or make up something. It's just that he didn't name two names of buyers, but only one. And now... he just started to feel like he should have come up with something more complicated.

- Are you opening it? I can even break down the door.

What an inopportune moment! What did it cost him to show up during the day? Now, probably, even the neighbors at the other end of the street can hear the screams at the porch.

Goslin pulled back the bolt and the door swung open with a kick from outside. It smelled of acrid smoke and blood. The stranger stepped through the threshold, and Goslin realized in horror why his outline looked so massive outside the window. The man, clearly having difficulty staying on his feet, carried a woman in a black dress, carefully wrapped in a patchwork blanket, thrown over his shoulder. Even worse, in the light of the lamp it became clear that on the guest's belt was hanging a sword with the well-known coat of arms of the city guard on the hilt. It was impossible to see his face behind his dirty hair, but for some reason Goslin immediately realized that it was unlikely that a real carrier of a lawman's weapon could look like this. A moment was spent pondering the situation—shouldn't he close the door from the outside and rush after the guards? But Goslin looked at the stranger and thought that he would not race with him.

"You said you weren't armed!"

"Close the door," the guest ordered.

The tone of the voice was such that Goslin, without any hesitation, quickly pulled the bolt with shaking hands and covered the window with the curtain. Behind him, the man swept away all the trash from the counter in one motion. The blanketed woman groaned as she was awkwardly picked up and lowered onto the polished tabletop. The blanket unfolded, Goslin recognized the witch Almasina in person.

"Good morning, Mister," she said quietly, trying to rise on her elbow, but immediately hissed in pain, pressing her palm to the torn and blood-soaked corset of her dress.

Goslin would have been glad to answer, but from fear his tongue stuck to the roof of his mouth.

"I got myself into trouble, as it is, I got into trouble!" — an alarming thought began to race in my head until the guest, without asking permission, dived into the depths of the shop with an unsteady step. You could hear floorboards creaking, doors opening, something knocking and rumbling. For some reason, Goslin had no desire to be outraged that his house was being left in disarray.

The witch somehow got up, leaning on her hand, and sat down. Her face was white, like that of a dead woman. Just above her head in the dim light could be seen the grinning skull of a damned boar.

- What's going on, Goslin? - asked the witch.

"I don't know," he answered honestly. - I don't know a thing.

- Is that so? Erevard Eagle Prim is dead, and for some reason someone decided that my potion was to blame. Did the guards come to you? Have you asked any questions?

- I do not know anything!

- Then why are you so afraid?

The man returned, carrying with him water collected in a copper basin, and some rags, which Goslin recognized as his torn sheets, washed only the day before by the washerwoman. The guest glanced at the owner of the house, seemingly only briefly, but Goslin shuddered in surprise. At first, the merchant thought this face was very familiar, but then he blinked and the obsession dissipated. Well, what kind of acquaintances can he have among the branded scum? The man turned around and looked straight at him with a strange, very unpleasant smile.

"Well, hello, buddy Allistir," he said.

Goslin nodded quickly. And he forced himself to stay in place, overcoming the instinctive desire to rush to the exit. Because now he definitely recognized this man. No one here could call him by his former name. Behind the man's back, the witch, not at all embarrassed, quickly unlaced the corset of her dress, freeing herself from the blood-soaked outerwear.

- Do you know him? — without any surprise she asked the man.

Although the question was not intended for him, Goslin shook his head in confusion.

"The limits of the Empire are narrow," said the man, too similar to Sir Thomas Wyatt, with the same smile. "The last time Allistir and I saw each other was ten years ago; he was a doctor and herbalist in Ernald Ash's retinue. However, it seemed to me then that all his manipulations were pure quackery and he traded better than he understood what he was selling.

"So, Thomas, this is definitely our mutual friend," the witch grinned.

Below the woman's collarbones there was a lacerated wound with burnt edges, which she was now trying to carefully wash. Pink water soaked the embroidered undershirt. Goslin knew what kind of object could leave such a mark, but that was not what worried him now.

"Can't be!"

Only when he caught the man's perplexed gaze did Goslin realize that he had said it out loud. The one who could not possibly be a hero of the war for freedom raised his eyebrows in surprise.

"Sir Thomas Wyatt is dead, killed by the Atarian conspirators," Goslin said.

The walking corpse nodded seriously.

- Certainly. And your master Ernald contracted the plague and died, am I right?

— Yes!

— A terrible disease, vile, insidious and completely unpredictable. Just yesterday the patient was standing on his feet and did not see a single symptom, but in the morning he simply did not get up, and by the evening he died completely.

- How do you know?

- To me? — Wyatt was amazed. - Out of nowhere, buddy. I just made a guess. Did you really guess right?

Goslin thought that he would not have time to remove the bolt again. But if you move to the side, closer to the door behind the counter, and seize the moment... The problem was that now Wyatt was not going to let him out of sight.

"I couldn't do something like that!" The gentleman was dear to me! - Goslin exclaimed in despair. - Whatever you think, I have nothing to do with it. Yes, there were some strange things. I felt that something wrong had happened. But what could I do? Who would believe me, who would stand up for me? Sir Yasen died, but I was alive and wanted to remain so in the future, so I just packed my things and quickly left the camp. I do not know anything!

Chuckling, Wyatt shook his head and looked at the witch.

- An excellent witness, don't you think? This guy doesn't even need to push hot needles under his nails. Just take a more stern look and he will say and do anything. I saw him briefly and a long time ago, so I think in this matter it is better to rely on your thoughts. Do you think he could have denounced you or somehow contributed to everything that happened today?

Realizing where everything was going, Goslin still took a cautious step to the side. Wyatt looked at him in such a way that the merchant's legs went numb. Pressing another clean piece of rag to the wound, the witch thought for a while, then slowly shook her head.

- Hardly. You see only part of the picture; in reality, everything is more complicated. There was no reason to tell you, but they started watching my house as soon as I brought you. Goslin cannot have a direct connection to this - we have not met, he could only know about the purchase from third parties, and even then it is unlikely. My thoughts on this matter are much sadder - it's my own fault. Already because I couldn't pass by.

Wyatt grinned evilly.

- Well, of course.

- I already tried to explain to you. The dead do not cause problems, but keeping the enemy alive is always fraught with some difficulties. Only if you are not going to use this life for some reason later. I could only suspect, but now I know for sure. You were the bait.

- What?

Goslin, deciding that now they had definitely forgotten about him in the heat of a difficult conversation, took two cautious steps towards the door. And then he felt someone's strong hand grab him by the scruff of the neck and push him, hitting his head on the nearest shelf. Painful, but not fatal - just as a warning.

-Where are you going, Allistir? Wyatt asked. "We're not done with you yet."

- A very revealing picture. The hero is in dire trouble. And put on public display," the witch continued to explain. - Anyone could have seen it. And already on the second day at the marketplace they were specifically looking for you. Who could it be, Thomas? Don't you understand yet? They really, really wanted to ransom you. It's just a pity that I managed to do it earlier, that's why I got caught. They obviously caught someone else with live bait. Right now, in this city. Otherwise it doesn't make sense.

Delving more and more into the conversation, Goslin began to fall into despair. Too much unnecessary dangerous information was dumped on his head. Meanwhile, the witch awkwardly tried to bandage herself; the man, with a calm expression, began to help. The spectacle became completely indecent, but no one seemed to pay attention to it.

- Why me? - asked Goslin.

He meant it angrily, but the tone of his voice came out very frightened.

After all, he had been dreaming of calm times for so long... And only recently did he cease to be afraid that someone who knew the past and would clean up the traces of an old crime would come after his soul. And now here he is - not even a mercenary sent by one of the current powers that be, but the real ghost of a long-dead knight. However, for a temporary guest from a place that sorcerers and witches call the Abyss, he looked too material and was clearly recently battered in some kind of mess. Goslin did not have the talent to communicate with ghosts, but he knew for certain that it would not be possible to beat one of them.

"It's unlikely they'll come up with a search for me here any time soon," said the witch. - There are no other reasons. I had no idea you had such a rich background, mister.

"I would prefer a long and quiet future for him," Goslin replied.

Wyatt chuckled.

- The only thing you always wanted was profit. He joined the camp while the case was winning, but as soon as a fleeting danger appeared, he ran away. Ash was a hero to you as long as he regularly paid you a generous salary. But the dead do not pay the living in hard cash, which is why you left the dead man in the care of conspirators and criminals. A good subject is the kind that enemies usually wish for.

"It's none of our business," said the witch. "Leave him alone, we need to decide what to do next."

- For what? This dog will immediately run to report everything to the guards, as soon as he gets distracted. First you need to decide what to do with it.

Goslin did not escape how Wyatt casually placed his palm on the hilt of someone else's sheathed sword. Try to scream, call for help? But the house has thick stone walls, and you can hardly expect help from your neighbors. The screams will only mean that he will die immediately.

"I'm not going to disturb you," Goslin spoke quickly. "I understand everything and I don't want to become your enemy." Take from me everything you need - I will only help. And I won't tell anyone anything. I swear!

Neither the witch nor the knight seemed at all impressed by the words.

"Okay," Goslin added. "If you don't trust me, you can tie me up and leave me." If you are afraid that I will immediately run for help, then I simply cannot do this.

Wyatt and the witch looked at each other.

- I do not like it. "This is unnecessary," she said as if she had read something in her companion's thoughts. - Don't do something that can be avoided. You yourself feel how everything is changing, right? Don't let it overwhelm you.

— Does the house have a basement? Wyatt asked.

Goslin himself brought his hands behind his back, allowing the former knight to tie his wrists tightly with the remnants of the torn sheets. It didn't even occur to the couple to search him. This fact cheered Goslin up a little. It's just a pity that he won't hear from the basement when the uninvited guests leave the house. You'll have to wait a little so as not to be caught off guard. Wyatt took him firmly by the elbow, and Goslin obediently walked, first deeper into the house, then along the narrow staircase, almost tripping on the chipped steps. He expected the man to simply let him go and slam the door, but together they reached the very bottom of the basement.

"Well... actually..." Goslin mumbled.

Wyatt grabbed him by the collar and stuffed the crumpled rag into his mouth, all the way down his throat. Goslin twitched, trying to spit out the gag that was choking him. And then he received a strong blow in the back, lost his balance and fell onto the floor littered with bags and boxes. Floundering among the debris, he only managed to see movement out of the corner of his eye - the man standing above him took his sword out of its sheath.

"Alas, luck smiles on rogues only occasionally," said Wyatt. "Sometimes you're lucky and money flows into your hands, sometimes you have to pay it yourself, sometimes even with your life."

Goslin tried to yell, but all that came out was a muffled grunt. Wyatt pulled his hair, forcing him to throw his head back.

"I dedicate the death of this traitor to Sir Ernald Big Ash, knight of the dead land, may his name remain famous for centuries." And may luck accompany me in battle.

Having uttered the ritual formula, Wyatt cut the merchant's throat.

* * *

Fifteen years ago

Sunlight streamed in from the stained glass window, and the floor was painted with bright spots of color. Thomas held an old book on his lap and carefully examined the illustration on the spread.

The library was never crowded, which is why he chose it as his main refuge in the palace.

Thomas was never able to fully understand why he was still alive. He was pardoned, and the last of the Wyatt family spent the next five moons in one of the palace towers, toiling from regrets and bad premonitions. He was given chambers that were much more luxurious than a prisoner would have been entitled to, but he was not allowed to leave them for too long for a free person. Oresia showed up to visit from time to time, had lengthy conversations and seemed to be looking closely to decide something important for herself. Then she said one day: "The Abyss has chosen you, you can become a sorcerer." Thomas believed it, although not immediately. From then on he was allowed to roam the palace freely.

The chronicle of sorcerers and witches said that the Abyss was nothing more than the underbelly of the human world. Magic comes from there through tiny gaps in reality to gift a random person at birth, to drop a tiny particle into his body. The human world is too rational to allow magical abundance, but the further away from cities and roads, the deeper the holes on the wrong side. A magical source may already seep into such ones. Or go through the original inhabitant of the Abyss, who wants to get acquainted with the world of people.

The book spread on the left side depicted the world of the White Sun, green hills and blue skies. At the edge of the leaf there is a gap, due to which a scaly monster emerges onto the ground, covered in soot from the daylight. On his back sits a naked woman with hair braided with ribbons. A witch, a frequent visitor to the underbelly of the world. So, in any case, he was told more than once. And still, something about this character alarmed Thomas. Behind the monster and his rider, on the right side of the spread, there is white dry grass and black, cracked earth, on which the shadows seem lighter than the falling rays of the Dark Sun. The world of witchcraft, gloomy, unkind to the children of the White Sun, appearing to them only in nightmares.

The more Thomas looked at the picture, the clearer the details of his own outlandish dreams became in his memory. He had seen them since childhood and always considered them some kind of fleeting stupidity. I wish I knew in advance what kind of stupidity would be decisive as a result...

Sounding footsteps were heard in the library hall. Thomas tensed, although he didn't show it. According to unspoken rules, he shouldn't be here. The imperial library was in the sole possession of Oresia. Even the ubiquitous retinue, more reminiscent of a pack of dressed up, ingratiating little dogs, and relentlessly following the mistress everywhere, was obliged to stay outside the threshold and not bother.

The repository was huge, it occupied an entire wing of the castle, and as soon as you took two dozen steps deeper into the labyrinth of shelves, it began to seem as if there was nothing left in the world except endless books. The cabinets were installed in any way, but not in the usual order, forming passages or dead ends in the most unexpected places, sometimes in the dark, sometimes with an elongated window, a table, a couple of armchairs. A whole dozen galleries loomed overhead, and everywhere there was the same thing - rows of spines, glass display cases with especially valuable rarities, again rows of spines. Probably every book created over the centuries, existing in the inhabited world and having important content or the richness of its binding, could be found here. If not the original, then at least an exact copy. Thomas suspected that, out of habit, one could get lost here and even die if the old caretaker for some reason did not want to save the library guest.

A whisper was heard approaching. It was impossible to make out the words, but Thomas knew that the same caretaker was probably already informing the hostess about the intrusion of an uninvited guest into her innermost territory. You could try to escape by sneaking into another side passage. Thomas sighed heavily, stretched out his legs, struggling with the frivolous desire to pile them into the chair opposite, and remained sitting.

The sound of footsteps meandered for a long time under the high arches, coming from one side and then from the other. Orecia seemed to have an excellent grasp of the labyrinth. However, Thomas thought with a grin, after so many years anyone would remember the road.

"What a pleasant surprise, Sir Wyatt."

"Your Highness," he responded, bowing his head slightly.

The woman approaching him now did not resemble "Highness" in any way. Orecia was dressed in a dress that was too simple for her usual formal wardrobe, and her hair was simply braided, without any hint of a complex hairstyle. The most ordinary, albeit very beautiful woman. Thomas, as usual, tried to notice some kind of discrepancy that would help destroy the illusion, but he could not - the face remained perfect, without a single hint of venerable age, although this simply could not be. In her hands, Oresia, like a diligent student, carried a stack of four books. READING K N I G O D. no

"We are glad that you managed to get comfortable here in such a short time," she said and, glancing briefly at the open book and clearly recognizing it, she added: "A very worthy choice, although we did not expect that you would be so interested in this area." arts What is your overall impression?

"Very entertaining," Thomas replied, trying to be polite.

However, looking at Orecia, he suddenly realized that this question was not at all part of the etiquette-based small talk, verbose and meaning nothing in essence.

- And what attracted your attention? - asked the Empress. - We are really interested.

Well, sincere interest was worthy of a sincere response.

"There are many stories collected here, and each tells its own story, each hero is looking for his own goal. Travels, finds adventures, risks his life, performs miracles. But after reading a dozen biographies, it is not difficult to understand the true desire of every sorcerer and every witch. I find it very funny the art with which this goal is decorated with adventures and exploits.

Orecia sank into the chair opposite.

"We are interested in what you saw here as our main desire."

- An indomitable thirst for power.

Her face did not change.

"A worthy conclusion," answered Orecia. "Although the tone inspires us that you see this as at least undignified, and most likely even disgusting."

- Rather, selfish and wasteful, if I may.

Orecia smiled wider.

- Why not? Let's allow it. Your straightforwardness is a delight to our ears.

"You can change the world," Thomas continued, not really knowing whether to perceive her answer as a barb or something else hidden behind it. "You have the power to stop epidemics, calm storms, turn deserts into blooming gardens. But you prefer to just intimidate people, hold their will and life in your hands and enjoy it.

Orecia was silent for some time, her gaze absent-mindedly glancing at the pattern of the stained glass window. And it seemed to Thomas that a strange change was happening to her. He could convince himself that this certainly couldn't be true. But the Witch Empress's face became sad for a while.

- The world can be changed, although time changes it without us. Human nature remains unchanged. We could talk about it for a long time, following the thinkers and philosophers who have been discussing it for centuries, but these words are empty words. We could convince, give arguments, but you will not understand us. The essence of a person is multifaceted; you can look at it all your life and not see the whole picture. There are questions the answer to which is valuable only if found independently. Therefore, it makes no sense for us to answer you by talking about magic and power. We will be able to talk about this only later, much later.

- And when? - Thomas asked, unable to contain his grin.

Orecia grinned too. And then she looked into his eyes and said:

— When the human essence splashes out on you like slop from a window on a warm sunny day, and you plunge into it from head to toe in your best outfit.

Part 11

Even on the first day, Thomas, to his own extreme displeasure, discovered that he was completely unaccustomed to staying in the saddle for a long time. The reason was quite serious - the day before he had been beaten thoroughly, even twice. The ribs under the tight bandage did not allow me to forget about myself for a moment. But in previous years, the inconvenience caused by one's own body was much easier to bear. The conclusion was disappointing. It's not that he became completely weak and sick, but such times will come one day. There may not be many years left.

On the first day, the witch also looked bad. She was unusually indifferent; she didn't even ask where he got those two horses that he brought to the shop just before dawn. Perhaps she guessed that she wouldn't like the answer. She silently changed into men's clothes and hid her long hair. And all this time Thomas thought that they would not get out of the city. The first detachment of guards will capture him, and what will happen then... His imagination generously imagined everything that would be done to him for aiding the witch. And the fact that the collar was removed from him, no matter how humiliating, only aggravated the situation - a free man, therefore, is obliged to answer for his misdeeds to the fullest extent. "No, don't, please, I can't stand it anymore!" - an invisible petty voice whined somewhere inside. He called to hide in the farthest corner, maybe even into the very basement where he left the murdered shop owner, just further away, deeper, and sit there, praying that the danger would pass. His whole nature resisted going out into the street and facing the threat.

Then Thomas made a wish - if his insight regarding his future fate was correct, then chance would take trouble away from him and help preserve his freedom and life. Took a deep breath. My hands were still trembling slightly, but a strange calm was already spreading in my soul.

They moved on horseback, making their way further and further west and staying away from the wide roads. The city of Recknitz stood on a hilly wasteland, slanting paths led sometimes uphill, sometimes downhill, exhausting the horses and their riders. At night, luckily there was no moon, I had to hide without lighting a fire in order to hide from the bandits living among the hills. However, either they were not noticed, or they simply decided that there was nothing to take from the two poor people and did not get involved.

In the morning, Thomas felt even worse than the day before. He got up using sheer willpower, simply forcing his collapsing body to move, found a narrow muddy stream, and wiped himself off with ice-cold water. It just got a little better. He watched gloomily as the witch bandaged the wound. The terrible inflammation subsided, and he once again thought that a human woman would not have been able to get out of such an altercation alive - she would have come down with a fever and burned to death. The witch looked indecently cheerful and full of energy, although she should have been greatly lacking the latter after the fiery performance in the city.

"But you've never been a person," he expressed a thought that had been bothering him for a long time. "Your chronicles say that experienced witches are able to penetrate the Abyss. But nowhere, probably intentionally, is it mentioned that they are capable of coming from there.

"It's just that these cases are so rare that mentioning them is not credible," was all she answered.

Soon they emerged from the hills onto the plain, and the road became more enjoyable.

- How did you find him? - he asked the witch only because the silence for some reason became burdensome.

- He was the one who found me. In fact, he has been here for a very long time. Sometimes hunters and their dogs wandered in to see him. But more often I had to lure the deer and roe deer myself. I didn't feed him, you shouldn't have decided so, I just accidentally caught his call when I went into the thicket in search of some kind of grass. I don't even remember what I was trying to find then. If it had been someone else in my place, the matter would have ended with a hearty dinner for the beast. But you have nothing to fear - I'll cover you. And the timing is good. When nature fades, he becomes drowsy. As long as you don't let yourself down.

"He himself".

The witch can help with something, but then she will leave, and Thomas will be left alone with the creation of the Abyss.

"When he sinks into your mind, you will feel as if you have become him." You will see everything that he knows. But only for a moment. Don't let yourself be charmed. You need a name and a symbol. Something that will separate you, something that will give you a chance to gain power from him and control it.

An inhabitant of the forest thicket has chosen a convenient crack in reality, like a predatory mollusk choosing a shell. If you let a monster grab you, you can get what he wants for himself more than anything else. Or remain forever lying under water in a world of white shadows and black light. It seemed to Thomas that the second outcome was the most likely, but for some reason the witch agreed to try her luck. Until this moment, he thought that he had almost guessed her intentions, but now... If the creature turns out to be too much for him, this woman will not even have the body of a failed servant left to repay the favor. Either she's too confident in him, or she's up to something. And here there could be no doubt about which option is correct.

On the third day, vast arable lands spread out before the eyes of the travelers. And the first prickly snowflakes suddenly fell from the gloomy sky.

It seemed to Thomas that he was about to fall out of the saddle. I begged myself to hold on a little longer and - what a miracle! - drove and drove. However, there were few supplies left by the witch, and this thought also inspired hope for a quick end to the torment. The riders went around the winter crops in a wide arc, crossed an abandoned field and finally approached the forest border. Very soon both had to dismount - the underbrush intertwined tight, whipping branches, trying to get at the worst, the ground, covered with white powder and last year's rotten leaves, hid ruts and holes, and even sharply fell down somewhere, threatening to break their legs. Overhead, in the tangle of half-naked branches, birds shouted anxiously to each other.

And then, at the end of the day, when there was only a little time left before sunset, they reached their goal.

Thomas first felt it and only then saw it. As if from his restless sleep, the silhouettes of gnarled trunks appeared towards him, opening a passage to a barely noticeable path. The trees are closely intertwined with their crowns overhead, forming a real ceiling vault with beams and branches. Underfoot, a patterned carpet of moss, untouched by anyone's footprints, spread with rare patches of whitened grass. It even seemed to Thomas for a while that he had entered a certain palace where forces lived that were too far from the human world. If you listened a little, you could even hear a broken whisper through the rustle of the wind in the falling leaves. Fatigue only supported the illusion. The voices spoke, a little warily, but with obvious curiosity, and if you make an effort to try to penetrate into the essence of their conversation...

"Zamri, five pagans!"

A rude shout pinned him to his place. Thomas blinked, shook his head, tearing the fabric of the ghostly disturbing vision, and found that he was standing a dozen steps from the place where he remembered himself last time, already among the dense thickets that scratched his face and hands into blood. The air blowing from the thickest black thicket carried the smell of water and wet stones. He could not see what was ahead in the slowly approaching twilight. I realized that I didn't want to look at it. So much so that I had to take my will into a fist and force myself to stay in place when I wanted to turn around and rush to run from there, where until recently I was so pulled by an invisible leash.

It turns out that during this time the witch managed to remove the saddle bags from her mare and was now moving towards him, leading the animal by the bridle.

"You insulted me," Thomas said.

- It's good that you began to notice this. It would hardly have turned out any other way. I screamed and called, and you walked.

She pushed her way through the thorny bushes, tugging at the mare's reins. She was as stubborn as she could, snoring and shaking her head. And the more sudden the change was. The horse froze, ears pricked. The witch affectionately stroked her on the withers and nudged her. The mare took off from her place and playfully rushed forward, breaking her way through the tangled branches, as if her beloved master or the best stallion in the whole world was waiting for her ahead. She was completely out of sight when the thicket brought echoing sounds - the splashing of water and a wild, frightened neighing. He was echoed by the melancholy voice of the remaining horse. For some time there, in the wilderness, there was a fierce battle. Then it became quiet. Even the birds fell silent.

Thomas felt the touch. The witch took his hand and squeezed his fingers for a brief moment, as if trying to wake him from his obsession.

- Here it is, your chance to change your mind.

He swallowed; his throat was dry and painful.

"You ruined our horse." As if only one will leave here.

"I saved your life, for a short time." It already senses that a person is here and is very hungry. We could have gone to bed, but I woke up already alone. The second horse will also have to be let down. Otherwise, you have no chance to return. Swallow it whole.

The sunset wind blew lightly, but pierced to the very bones. Thomas didn't want to think that it was actually primal fear, gnawing at his aching, tired body.

"Help us collect branches, let's make a fire," the witch suggested.

- But I must...

- You should do this no earlier than in the morning. It takes some time. Are you tired.

While he was collecting brushwood, the witch got rid of the second horse, letting it go into the thicket.

Later, already sitting by the fire, on a bed of a spread out cloak and chopped fir branches, drinking the last of the drink from the flask, feeling the cozy heat pouring into his face, Thomas thought that at his age, his father, at the head of the army, united six provinces, turning real barbarians into the most formidable force in the Great North. He sent flotillas of warships overseas, increasing wealth and military glory. How would he look at his son, driven away to the capital, wearing a slave collar and now serving the main enemy of the clan? He probably wouldn't even bother to spit in his face. Thomas failed all his expectations, one after another. What's the difference now? The time of great kingdoms has passed, the world is breaking up into provinces, spreading deep into lands that were previously considered wild and ruinous. On the main throne sits the one who sacrificed to the goddess-glory all who were his associates, friends, brothers. The witch hinted that there were still faithful people left, but what did he need them for? He won't be able to protect them.

— Thomas...

He looked up. On the other side of the fire, a witch sitting on the ground was taking off her clothes. A jacket, a frock coat, a belt... She pulled off her boots, stood up and walked over to him, stepping on the hot coals rolling on the ground.

- Why are you so sad, Thomas?

It's strange, he thought, men's clothing usually looks ridiculous on women, but it suits this one. Although, what kind of woman is she...

She sat down next to him, snuggled up, resting her head on his shoulder.

"Perhaps I can distract you from bad thoughts?"

"Don't forget who she is," whispered an inner voice, now no louder than a light breeze over the field.

Warmth emanated from her body, gentle, soothing. I should have pushed her away, but that would have taken too much strength. Thomas felt all the weariness of recent years fall upon him. It was as if all this time his body had been tense in a spasm, and now the spasms had ended, and pain had come in the overstrained muscles. Someone else's warmth drove her away.

- What are you doing? - he asked, and his tongue slurred like a drunken one.

"I'm trying to help you fulfill your part of the contract, brave knight." I want to take it now.

- While I'm still alive? - he muttered.

She tried to help him get rid of excess clothes, although it turned out to be extremely awkward, then she leaned on him, knocking him onto his back, and Thomas did not resist. He collapsed on the mat, smelling the fire, fir branches, and a hot female body. She climbed on top of him...

"I was so looking forward to this, Thomas... it's so sad that enmity and death came between us." It pained me so much to know that you thought I had come to torment you. You are a good person, I like you, I couldn't do this just because I owe you revenge for my own murder...

Through half-closed eyelids, Thomas watched the slow, measured movement. He stretched out his hands and found soft flesh yielding to his touch. Something long-forgotten woke up inside and felt a painful languor. He moved towards her, no longer feeling any heaviness or pain, squeezed her with both hands, forcing her to freeze, then he moved towards her. With a quiet groan, she accepted the increasing rhythm imposed on her. And so, squeezing her in his arms, Thomas looked into someone else's dark eyes, and a hot wave pierced right through him. The witch had no eyes. Instead of them, a black haze swirled.

"Rivers of blood in the gorges of city streets..." she muttered in an alien, low, dull voice. — The trampled nobility thirsts for blood. A trampled fire becomes poisonous smoke.

Without remembering himself, Thomas grabbed her, turned her over, crushed her under him, not paying attention to weak attempts at resistance. The witch fell to the mat, scratching the ground as if trying to crawl away.

"Well, no," he declared hoarsely, "she wanted to be my mistress...

"You will have a mistress, you will have a wife," the witch continued, as if answering him, "and the roses in her hands will be black, and there will be dust in her chest." Her name will be Death.

Thomas leaned harder and grabbed him by the hair, forcing him to throw his head back. A painful groan was heard. And he liked it. He pulled again, squeezed his trembling throat with his palm to feel how the vibration of someone else's voice was transmitted to his body, causing waves of painful goosebumps. And he moved faster, feeling that very soon, just a little more...

It took him a while to come to his senses. And he lay there for a long time, looking at the pattern of branches above his head, illuminated by the red flame of the fire, and the rare snowflakes that made their way through the arches of the forest palace and slowly swayed in the chilly air. The witch was nearby. She pressed her whole body tightly against him, as if she was trying to maintain the warmth of the embrace. And the thoughts in my head were surprisingly clear.

"You mixed something in the flask." And she herself accepted some nasty thing. From all this that you said...

- What did I tell you? - the witch was wary.

He felt he had to shut up and just shook his head. Raising herself on her elbow, she looked into his face, looking for something in his eyes for a long time and carefully. Thomas thought he could kiss her to distract her. Fortunately, she relaxed herself and lay down again, resting her head on his shoulder.

There was a long silence. Thomas fell asleep.

Opening his eyes the next time, he found a bright cloudless sky above him, covered with a network of branches. The witch slept so soundly, as if her spirit had temporarily left her body. Thomas got out of the embrace, wrapped a cloak around the naked female body, and began to quickly get dressed. I pulled on my underwear and realized that the rest would be unnecessary. In water, clothes will become wet and heavy, hindering movement.

— Thomas?..

The call, barely louder than a whisper, made him flinch. The witch's eyes were half closed. She moved weakly, but did not even try to get up.

"Thomas," she called again.

He could have simply backed down and left. But, not understanding himself, he bent over the mat, looking into the pale, haggard face. The witch smiled faintly and reached out, clearly intending to touch his cheek with her palm. But she stopped the movement. The hand fell, as if suddenly filled with heaviness, and the eyes closed.

Thomas got up and walked away, into the depths of the thickets, protected by sharp branches of bushes. Then they parted and the man stepped out onto the withered grass.

It was no longer snowing, the sky cleared. There was probably a flooded river nearby. The land here sloped downward and sank into the water. The grass stems swayed in the muddy thickness, like real algae. Thomas hesitated only a moment. And he managed to feel the unbearable weight that he had been carrying on his shoulders all the past days. The weight of endless and unbearable disappointment. This is how the shadow of the great parent must have looked at him if she had appeared at the forest fire last night.

Of all the things he ever wanted, the main value was justice. He thought so. And I realized late that I had been deceived. I was deceived myself, with joy, with youthful delight. Like anyone brought up on ballads about the exploits of their ancestors, they dreamed of defeating the monster and saving as many lives as possible. Having lost his family, clan, and all lands, he received the power capable of changing the world. And even defeated his dragon. But why did the short-lived allies appoint him as the next dragon? Was it because he was too strong for them?

He was strong, but he tried to pretend that he was not worth fearing. What stupidity! This is the facet of human essence - he experiences fear of an element that is more powerful than him. It is human nature to deal with any threat. And Thomas gave in and showed his own vulnerability. While he himself was thinking about how to remain humane, someone behind his back was deciding how to use humanity against him.

Now he knows a little more so as not to repeat the previous mistake. He will have only one chance to correctly answer the question - what does he really want?

Grass and whitish autumn flowers swayed in the darkness at the bottom, and Thomas took the first step. Then another one, and another. The water was not cold, it accepted him like a heated river on a southern summer afternoon. It was warmer than the air that penetrated the skin like icy needles. Small ripples washed over his knees when Thomas felt the first gentle touch on his ankle. But something hiding behind the long stems of grass only briefly touched him and retreated. Sensing a trap, the victims try to escape. And the man just stood there and took another step. This alarmed the creation of the Abyss.

- Well, what are you doing? Come to me, don't you see, I'm a simple person, I'm nothing before you...

He walked, the water rose towards him. She almost touched the belt when something grabbed it and pulled. Thomas clenched his teeth and, without even uttering a frightened cry, fell into the water. Slippery vines moved there, they first wrapped around his legs, then grabbed his arms, desperately rushing in search of support. They entangled his body, hips, shoulders, neck, not allowing him to move, and then he clearly realized that he was about to die.

"Don't let yourself be charmed. You need a name and a symbol," whispered a gentle voice.

Thomas tensed, trying to fight. He felt a monstrous grip and at the same time contemplated himself from the side, drowning and twitching in the bonds of black vines. An unknown force tied him hand and foot, and held him under water, not allowing him to escape. But I saw that the light overhead was slowly moving away. Primitive darkness closed in all around. The bottom was covered with intertwining black vines and piles of white sharp bones. And something was still pulling his helpless body to the depths, without releasing the suffocating grip.

And he felt this grip as if he himself was holding a barely warm life in his long, nimble fingers.

When he last saw the sky behind the muddy curtain of water, it was black, and white tree branches intertwined against it. And then a black light flashed in his head, and the world ceased to exist.

"What do you want? What are you looking for here?

He no longer had a body, a mind, no past or future, he overflowed, turning into warm water, and he slid, writhing in the water with black flexible vines. But he knew the answer to this question.

"Power".

And the word turned into a silver blade, cutting the darkness with deadly lightning. And in the blinding light, Thomas saw a symbol.

Part 12

When the barely audible steps and rustling of parted branches died down, Gilota again raised her hand and looked at the ring with the red stone turned towards her palm. There was still enough deadly poison left on the sharp edges. But she was unable to make the decisive move and bring death to the man with whom she spent the night.

She lay there, listening, and realized that the sensations in her body had strangely changed. This could never happen to a human woman, everything is different with them. And now she knew for sure that a new life, still weak, like a spark from a fire, but already flaring up brighter, had arisen inside. The flow of power in her veins changed direction, feeding a new source. One cycle of existence has given way to another, and very soon the stars in the sky and the spirits of the Abyss will begin to predict new bloody upheavals for the world.

Before, Gilota did not know why her mother released her into the world with this curse of eternity inside. She even hated her for it. When things got really hard, she would stoop to cursing her and calling on the most terrible punishments of the Abyss on her head. She fell into despair when the irresistible flow carried her to another inevitable death. And every time she thought that her mother had experienced this feeling over and over again. And she was just as sick, and she hated just as much, until she became the one who calmly perceived any manifestation of the outside world, and even gave this world her daughter. What could have motivated the witch in committing this madness?

Now her time had come, and Gilota knew the answer. The force told her. What she burned into herself was still full, pouring over the edge, threatening to one day tear it apart. The force hinted that it had become too much. The force left no other choice. Share.

Is this why her mother was always so cold? She didn't want to either. And I also didn't find any other way out. One cycle of existence gives way to another. Every living creature must leave offspring, and wise nature knows how to push this creature to the right decision.

There was very little time left. She tried with Raven, but he was unsuitable. Too human. The human element prevailed in him, no matter how much strength Gilota tried to pour into him, expecting that they would take root and become part of his nature.

And then life itself presented her with a suitable vessel.

Gilota listened, trying to discern approaching footsteps among the sounds of the forest. But no, it's too early.

Will he know that she took advantage of him? For sure.

Is she afraid of this? Not at all.

After all, he also deceived her.

The witch is able to remember her visionary visions. She knows what she told him at night, sitting astride his hips, but being in spirit in the Abyss.

The trampled nobility thirsts for blood.

This man was a hero, but he turned out to be unnecessary to the people he was trying to stand up for. He was destroyed, but returned from the dead to be changed forever. And Gilota, alas, saw fully how he had changed. And how he will have to change in the future. But... she was interested in looking at this transformation up close. In her many lifetimes, she had never encountered anything like this. A hero who wanted to save this world with the same passion with which he would now begin to destroy it.

Hastily dressing in a man's suit from someone else's shoulder, she swept away the coals of the fire and scattered cut spruce branches into the thickets. She gathered her things into bags and, putting the luggage on her shoulder, trudged through the thickets. There was nothing more sinister here - the owner of the water was too busy. So Gilota sat down in the grass and waited. The dim autumn sun slowly crept across the sky. Gilota barely moved.

She has always been alone, but that will soon change.

Something dark and seething was rising towards her from the depths. A continuously moving lump of black vines splashed onto the shore and flowed away again, leaving a prostrate human body on the ground. Gilota rushed to him, fell to her knees next to him, peering into his frozen face. Absolutely clean, devoid of scars and marks of time. And then the man suddenly opened his eyes, rolled over to his side and coughed, releasing muddy dark water from his insides.

- Thomas! - she called him.

He wanted to answer, but only burst into another coughing fit. Then he finally overcame himself, took a deep breath and said hoarsely:

- Greetings, Gilota.

She shuddered because she had never told him her real name. And the one who was called Thomas raised his head and smiled, the sparks of darkness brought from the Abyss slowly extinguished in his eyes. The grass smoldered under his fingers.

"Happy birth to you, brother Thomas," Gilota told him.